CHA...
DREAM

BY
JENNIFER TAYLOR

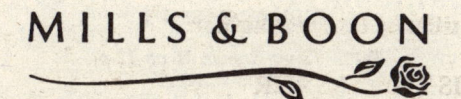

MILLS & BOON

MILLS & BOON LIMITED
ETON HOUSE, 18-24 PARADISE ROAD
RICHMOND, SURREY TW9 1SR

DID YOU PURCHASE THIS BOOK WITHOUT A COVER?

If you did, you should be aware it is **stolen property** as it was reported *unsold and destroyed* by a retailer. Neither the Author nor the publisher has received any payment for this book.

All the characters in this book have no existence outside the imagination of the Author, and have no relation whatsoever to anyone bearing the same name or names. They are not even distantly inspired by any individual known or unknown to the Author, and all the incidents are pure invention.

All Rights Reserved. The text of this publication or any part thereof may not be reproduced or transmitted in any form or by any means, electronic or mechanical, including photocopying, recording, storage in an information retrieval system, or otherwise, without the written permission of the publisher.

This book is sold subject to the condition that it shall not, by way of trade or otherwise, be lent, resold, hired out or otherwise circulated without the prior consent of the publisher in any form of binding or cover other than that in which it is published and without a similar condition including this condition being imposed on the subsequent purchaser.

MILLS & BOON and the Rose Device are trademarks of the publisher.

First published in Great Britain 1994 by Mills & Boon Limited

© Jennifer Taylor 1994

Australian copyright 1994   Philippine copyright 1994 This edition 1994

ISBN 0 263 78551 3

Set in Times Roman 10 on 12 pt. 01-9407-54286 C

Made and printed in Great Britain

CHAPTER ONE

It was the man's hair that caught her attention first. Thick and vibrant, it gleamed like burnished copper under the hot Florida sun. Add to that a leanly muscled six-foot-plus frame, and an aura of power and confidence, and the result was, frankly, devastating!

Stephanie let her eyes linger appreciatively on the man a moment longer, then realised she was in danger of missing the very thing she'd come to see. Mickey, Donald, Goofy...all her childhood favourites were about to pass a few feet away, and the man was blocking her view of the parade.

She edged sideways, aiming for a small gap to the man's left, then gasped when someone jogged her elbow, sending the large-size cup of frosted cola she'd just bought flying from her hand. It hit the man's broad back and splattered in every direction, spilling dark brown liquid all over the back of his white T-shirt and the seat of his jeans. For a stunned second Stephanie just stared at the damage, then hurriedly pulled a handful of tissues from her bag and tried to wipe up the mess.

'I'm really sorry,' she muttered apologetically, mopping at the stain spreading across the man's muscular back. 'It was just an accident, but...'

He caught her hand as he turned to glare at her, his face like stone, his eyes mirroring displeasure, and she felt the words dry up. His eyes were very dark, bitter-chocolate-brown, under brows the same colour, his face deeply tanned. With hair that colour his skin should have been pale, his eyes...

'Blue, definitely blue,' she heard herself murmur, and flushed to the roots of her dark brown hair with embarrassment.

'I beg your pardon?' His voice was very deep, gravelly, and so unfriendly that Stephanie gulped. She dragged her hand away from his grasp and bent back to the stain, wiping the wad of tissues down the back of his muscular thigh before suddenly realising exactly what she was doing. She straightened abruptly, her face beet-red, her soft blue eyes filled with apology.

'I really am sorry. It was just an accident, you see. Someone behind me jogged my arm and——'

He cut her off, his expression never softening at the sincerity with which she offered her apologies. 'Forget it. It really doesn't matter.'

How could anyone with eyes that colour make them look so cold? The thought skipped through her mind almost too fast for her to be aware of it before she realised that the man was moving away from her. She couldn't let him go like that, not until she'd at least offered to pay for any damage she'd caused to his obviously expensive clothing. She followed him through the crowd, murmuring apologies to left and right for the disturbance she was causing.

'But Dad, we'll miss it now! Can't we just stay until the parade goes past and then go back so you can change?'

She hadn't realised he had anyone with him before, and now she slowed, studying the pleading face of the little girl whom he was holding firmly by the hand. It was obvious even without having heard what the child had called him that she was his daughter, because she had the same glorious colour hair surrounding a face that was just a shade too pale and wan for a child her age. As Stephanie hovered uncertainly, the man glanced down at the child, his expression softening just for a moment.

'We can come back, Jess. There's another parade later on, and we can watch that. I can't stay here in these clothes. I'm soaked to the skin, thanks to that fool woman back there.'

Fool woman! Just who did he think he was calling a 'fool woman'? It had been an accident, pure and simple, and anyone with a spark of decency would have accepted her apology in the spirit it had been intended! She pivoted on her heel, all thoughts of making further apologies or offers to pay to have his clothes cleaned fading abruptly at his boorishness, but she'd gone no more than a step or two when the child spoke again, a hint of tears in her voice that brought Stephanie to a halt.

'Oh, but that's not fair! If we go back now then you'll find something more important to do rather than come back here, and you promised, Daddy. You promised!'

'I know I did. And I have every intention of sticking to that promise. Now come along.'

'No! I won't. I want to stay here!'

'What you want, young lady, is——'

She'd heard enough, more than enough. It was her fault that the child's day was being ruined, although she could have expected the man to show a bit more understanding towards his daughter. From the sound of it, the little girl had set her heart on seeing the parade.

'Excuse me, I couldn't help overhearing what was going on, and I wonder...' She faltered as the man turned slowly towards her. There was something frankly intimidating about his height, the sheer breadth of his muscular shoulders straining under the thin cotton, the iciness of those disturbingly dark eyes. For a moment Stephanie almost forgot what she'd been trying to say, before hurriedly marshalling her thoughts again. 'I was wondering if I could help in some way.'

He raised a mocking brow, his thin lips curving into a faint smile that seemed closer to a sneer. 'Help? I think you've already done more than enough today, thank you.'

Stephanie flushed, but she stood her ground, refusing to back down in the face of such open hostility. She shot a quick look at the child's unhappy face and drew her strength from that. No child that age should look so unhappy in Disney's Magic Kingdom. It was a contradiction in terms that she couldn't accept!

'I have apologised already for what happened, but perhaps you didn't hear me before,' she said sweetly, staring steadily back at him. 'So let me repeat myself. I am extremely sorry. It was an accident, but that can't be much consolation for you. The one thing I don't want to happen, though, is that your daughter should suffer because of it.' She smiled warmly at the child and received a small, hesitant smile in return. 'If you would like to go back to your hotel to change, then I shall be only too pleased to mind your daughter for you until you get back. That way she won't have to miss any of the day.'

'Dad, d'you think——?' The faintly hopeful note in the child's voice was drowned out by deeper tones, tones that sent a shudder of ice inching slowly down Stephanie's backbone despite the heat of the July sun.

'My daughter won't miss anything. Thank you for your offer of help, but I'm afraid I shall have to turn it down.'

He didn't sound sorry—in fact he didn't sound even the tiniest bit concerned that she must have heard the scorn in his refusal—and for some reason it didn't really surprise her. Whoever he was, this man wouldn't care one way or the other about people's opinions of him. He was a man who lived by his own rules, not by those written by others.

Stephanie was sorely tempted to turn tail and walk away from the open hostility, but a quick glance at the child's disappointed face stopped her. She took a deep, heartening breath and tried again to get through to him. 'I realise that you must be wary of letting a stranger take charge of your daughter, but I assure you she will be perfectly safe. I have identification if you would like to see it.' She opened her bag, then jumped when his hand closed over hers, his fingers hard and dry against hers.

'Don't bother. I don't want to see any ID because I don't intend to take you up on your offer.' His eyes skimmed her slender body with an insulting thoroughness, lingering on the thrust of her breasts under the sleeveless lime-green T-shirt before travelling down her rounded hips to her long legs, bare under the hem of her lime and navy shorts. 'I might have been flattered if it hadn't been so obvious, honey. Unlike a lot of men nowadays, I prefer to do the chasing myself. I guess I must be a bit old-fashioned like that.'

'I... Pardon?' It came out as a whisper of horror as what he meant hit home with the force of a sledgehammer. For a moment Stephanie could only stand and stare at him, wishing there was something she could think of to say to wipe the arrogant smile off his equally arrogant face.

'Don't take it to heart too much, will you?' He shrugged indolently, letting his hand drop away from hers before he glanced down at the child by his side. 'I'm sure that some guys would appreciate your interest, but if you'll take my advice then I suggest you modify it somewhat next time. It can be off-putting to have that amount of Coke thrown over you.'

'Now you just look here. I never...!' Her voice tailed off as she suddenly realised she was speaking to thin air. She took a deep breath, glaring at the man's broad back as he made his way through the crowd. She had never met anyone so arrogant and self-opinionated and full of himself in the whole of her twenty-five years! It was a wonder he could manage to walk with an ego that big weighing him down! That he should imagine for even a moment that she'd spilled her drink over him deliberately... Well!

Fuming, she turned back to the crowd lining the roadside, but her heart really wasn't in watching the parade now. She glanced at her watch, wondering if she should call it a day and return to her hotel, but if she did that then she would miss her one and only chance to see this very special piece of Disney World magic. She was on a very tight schedule, with every one of the next three days filled: Epcot, Sea World, Universal Studios, all to be seen and reported on when she got back to England and met up with Laura and Rachel again. The trip had been her idea; she'd cajoled the other two into coming along, confidently dismissing any worries they'd had about giving up their jobs to take six months off to see Europe, culminating in a few days in Florida to enjoy all the man-made attractions.

They had been friends in university and kept in contact afterwards, Stephanie and Laura both opting for careers in teaching, while Rachel had gone into social work. It was a shame the trip hadn't worked out quite as planned, what with Laura staying on in Spain and Rachel receiving the news that her father had suffered a stroke just hours before she and Stephanie were due to board the flight to America. It was at Rachel's insistence that she had agreed to carry on with the plan, so was she really going to let that man spoil it for all of them?

Her chin lifted and she pushed back into the crowd to watch the glitzy parade passing, and if thoughts of that arrogant redhead did occasionally slip into her mind then she quickly dismissed them. That was one bit of Florida she didn't want any reminders of to take home!

The night was soft and balmy. Stephanie side-stepped a family group of mother, father and three excited children, almost tempted to follow them, but she'd done every single attraction and she didn't think her aching feet could take much more. It was already after eight o'clock, way past the time that she'd planned to return to her hotel. Tempting though the thought of staying for another hour or so was, she had to get back or she would be too tired to enjoy Epcot in the morning.

With a last reluctant glance over her shoulder she started back towards the exits and the bus that would take her back to her hotel. After all these months travelling, funds were running low, so she hadn't been able to afford the cost of hiring a car for her stay. However, she'd been lucky enough to find a hotel at Lake Buena Vista which ran a courtesy bus service to all the Disney attractions, so that hadn't proved to be a problem.

She rounded a corner, then slowed when she noticed the child standing forlornly at one side of the path. There was something vaguely familiar about her, but it wasn't until she shifted into the light spilling from a nearby hot-dog cart that Stephanie recognised her. Even as Stephanie hesitated, the little girl took a look around then started to cry, fat tears sliding down her pale cheeks.

Stephanie hurried forwards and crouched down beside her. 'What's the matter, love?' She searched her memory and came up with the echo of a deep, gravelly voice, quickly stemming the accompanying shiver that ran down her spine. 'It's Jess, isn't it? I spoke to your daddy before... remember?'

The child sniffed, wiping a hand across her face as she stared back at Stephanie. 'It's Jessica Alice, and I do remember. Daddy called you "that fool woman" and was awfully cross all the way back to the hotel.'

Stephanie hid a grimace. 'Jessica Alice is a nice name. Mine is Stephanie Jacobs. So tell me what's wrong, Jessica. Have you hurt yourself?' She put her bag down beside her on the path and pulled out a tissue to wipe the child's face, then smiled at her reassuringly.

Jessica shook her head, her blue eyes tear-sodden as they stared back at Stephanie.

'Then what is the matter?' Stephanie glanced round. 'Are you by yourself? Where's your daddy?'

'He's gone!' the child wailed. 'He said he wouldn't be long, but he's not come back. He's left me!'

The child's distress was evident, her choice of words somehow disturbing. Stephanie frowned, tossing the statement around her head to see what it was that bothered her about it before shrugging the idea aside. Naturally a child this age would be upset at being separated from her parent. She caught hold of the little girl's hand and held it firmly, making her voice as deliberately reassuring as she could. 'That's the trouble with daddies; they will go wandering off on their own and getting lost. I expect he's feeling just as scared and miserable right now.'

'Is he?' Jessica glanced up at her, her face very solemn.

'Of course. I mean, being on your own among all these people... Why, even the biggest daddy would be scared.'

Jessica smiled shyly. 'I don't think my daddy is scared of anything.'

Amen to that, Stephanie silently endorsed. That man would be the one to do the scaring, not vice versa! However, she kept the thought to herself and smiled back at the child. 'Even the biggest, toughest people get scared sometimes, chick.'

Jessica giggled. 'I'm not a chick. Hens have chicks.'

Stephanie ruffled the silky red curls on top of her head and grinned. 'Where I come from that just means...well, honey or dear. OK?'

'OK.' The child glanced round, and her mouth started to droop again. 'Daddy still isn't here. He's left me.'

'Now why on earth should you imagine he's done that?'

Jessica shook her head, staring down at the toes of her trainers as two tears slid down her cheeks. Stephanie stared at her helplessly. She'd never seen a child cry this way, silently, and it bothered her. She looked round at the crowds milling around them and came to a sudden decision, realising that she had to do something. 'Look,

Jessica, shall we walk down this path and see if we can find your daddy for you? If we can't then we can go and find one of the people who work here, and maybe they will announce it over the speakers that you've been found and where your dad can come to collect you.'

'But what if he doesn't come?' She clung to Stephanie's hand, her small fingers gripping painfully hard. 'You won't leave me here, will you?'

There was something most definitely wrong here, but now wasn't the time to speculate on it. She bent down and gave the girl a quick hug, then straightened and looked her in the eyes. 'I won't leave you on your own, love. I promise. Now come along. The sooner we find your father, the better.' And the sooner I can give him a piece of my mind, she thought, but was wise enough not to say it aloud. The man had to be careless to a fault to let his daughter get lost like this.

They walked along the path, Stephanie doing her best to stave off the child's tears by telling her amusing little stories about her trip, and even about the year she'd spent teaching after she'd left college, but finally she was forced to admit that they were achieving nothing. With these crowds they could have passed Jessica's father a dozen times and not seen him. Taking a firmer grip on the girl's hand, she turned along a side-path, following the sign for the information office.

'And where do you think you are going with my daughter?'

There was such anger in those gravelly tones that they would have stopped her in her tracks even if she hadn't recognised them instantly. Stephanie swung round, her heart turning over at the sight of the tall red-haired man who was standing just behind them, his face set into grim lines that boded ill for her.

'Daddy! You came back for me. You didn't leave me!' The child's shout seemed to get through to him, bypassing the naked fury on his handsome face. He bent and scooped her up, hugging her quickly before setting her back on her feet. 'Go and sit down on that bench over there, Jess. And don't move...understand? That's how you got lost last time, by not doing as you were told.'

The child kicked at a stray petal that had dropped on to the path but did as she was told, sitting down on the bench just out of earshot. Stephanie watched her, then looked back at the man, taking a quick step back as he moved almost menacingly towards her.

'Just what kind of a game are you playing, lady? What were you doing with my daughter?'

His voice was rough with anger, his eyes dark with it, and Stephanie flinched. 'I...I wasn't doing anything! Well, I guess that isn't quite true.'

He smiled dangerously, lessening the distance between them to less than a foot, far too close for her peace of mind. Suddenly she could almost feel the heat of his big, powerful body, smell the scent of his skin—a tangy, heady mixture of soap and man—and her heart gave a sudden shocking little leap, then started to beat a fraction faster.

'I'm sure it isn't...true,' he added when she looked at him with a total lack of comprehension. 'So what were you up to?'

'I...' She licked her dry lips, then felt colour sear her cheeks when she saw the way his eyes traced the action before lifting to hers with a faint gleam in their dark depths. Anger surfaced inside her, hot and furious; he thought she'd done that deliberately, as some kind of blatant come-on! Why of all the egotistical, self——

'Cat got your tongue, lady? Or don't you feel like making any explanations to me right now?' He shrugged lightly. 'That's fine by me. You can always talk to the police. I'm sure they will be only too interested in why you were attempting to abduct my child.'

Enough was enough! She stood up straighter, trying to stare him in the eyes, an impossible task in view of her five feet seven inches compared to his six feet plus. 'You can stop right there before you go any further. I found your daughter crying because you'd lost her. I was trying to find the lost children collection point when you came across us.'

He barely glanced at the sign she was pointing to, his eyes boring coldly into hers. Brown eyes were meant to be warm and friendly, so how had he managed to perfect this trick of making them look colder than snow on a winter's day? She shook herself out of the musing reverie, aware that she hadn't heard a single word he'd said.

'I beg your pardon?'

'I asked where you found her. If it isn't too difficult a question for you to answer.'

She flushed at the open sarcasm. 'On the path back there, near a hot-dog stand.' Her chin lifted, unconsciously regal, as she stared back at him. 'I can't imagine how any caring parent could lose a child that age.'

He bent slightly, staring into her face. 'I didn't lose her. I told her to stay right there until I got back.'

'Oh! I see. But why leave her in the first place, especially here when it's so busy? It seems like a totally irresponsible thing to do.'

'Almost as irresponsible as your taking her away? For your information, Miss Do-gooder, I couldn't take her where I was going.' He smiled tightly. 'In case you haven't noticed, she's a girl and I'm a man. There are one or two places where I just can't take her... like the restroom, for instance.'

Oh, she'd noticed that he was a man all right; how could she have missed noticing that? Her traitorous eyes did a quick survey of the very masculine lines of his body before coming back to his face with an awareness in them which she couldn't quite hide and which she knew immediately he understood.

He smiled slowly, confidently, obviously aware of the effect he had on women. 'I see that you understand. Good. Maybe you won't repeat your mistake now.'

He turned to walk away, but Stephanie caught his arm, her fingers tightening around the iron-hard flesh. 'Look, I'm sorry if you feel this has been my fault, but you have to try to understand the situation I was put in. Jessica was extremely upset when I came across her. She seemed to think that you'd left her and that you weren't coming back.'

Something crossed his face, some emotion so raw that it was almost painful to watch. But then his expression smoothed out again into the sardonic lines she was growing to recognise. 'But I did come back, didn't I? So this is no longer your problem. Goodnight.'

'And that's it, is it? You're just going to walk off without a word of thanks? I didn't have to waste my time by staying with her.'

He glanced down at where her hand held his arm, then looked back straight into her face with a smile that chilled her to the bone. 'Then why did you, honey? Were you hoping for some sort of... reward?' His tone was little short of insulting, and Stephanie dropped her hand from him at once as though he had struck her.

'No! You have a nerve, Mr...' She stopped abruptly, but he said nothing, merely watched her, and she rushed on, 'I don't want any reward, and definitely nothing along the lines you mean! Frankly, I pity that poor child having you for a father!'

For a moment she thought he was going to strike her. His anger was so great, almost tangible as it scorched the air between them. Then with a staggering show of self-discipline he brought himself under control. He walked over to the bench and took Jessica's hand, then turned to glance over his shoulder at where Stephanie was still standing. 'One word of free advice, and that is to keep your opinions to yourself when you have no idea what you're talking about. It could save you a whole lot of trouble, believe me.'

'I know enough about children to recognise when something is wrong!'

'Frankly, lady, I don't give a damn what you know or don't know! Goodnight.'

He started to walk away, but the child hung back, then suddenly broke free and came rushing back to hug Stephanie, her small arms locking tightly around the woman's slim hips.

'Thank you for taking care of me, Stephie. I wish you could do it all the time!'

Startled, Stephanie dropped to one knee and hugged her back, holding the little body close against her own for a moment before slowly putting the child from her. 'It was my pleasure, Jessica, but now I think it's time you went. Your daddy is waiting for you.'

She glanced over the child's head at the tall man who was standing a few feet away and felt something inside her start to ache at the expression on his face. Just for a moment their eyes met in a look that seemed to cut straight to her heart, then he called the child to him and turned to walk away without another word.

Stephanie stood up slowly, and took a long breath, feeling more upset than she could explain. He was just an arrogant, overbearing male, so why did she feel like sitting down and weeping when she remembered that expression of regret and pain in those devil-dark eyes? She had no idea, just the certainty that he wouldn't thank her for feeling that way!

CHAPTER TWO

'I'M AFRAID that's all we can do for now, ma'am. The police have been informed, and naturally we shall contact you immediately if it turns up. We operate a very strict security code here which keeps crime to a minimum, but...' The young man shrugged expressively, not needing to voice the rest of what he'd been thinking. Stephanie knew exactly what it was and couldn't blame him. How could she have been so careless as to leave her bag lying on the path like that? Even allowing for the fact that she'd been concerned about helping Jessica, it had been an incredibly stupid thing to do.

She smiled her thanks at the man behind the desk, then left the office, trying to stave off the almost overwhelming panic she felt, but it was hard to control it. That bag had contained everything—passport, credit cards and nearly every cent. Now what was she going to do?

Wearily she made her way to the bus-stops, wondering how she was going to get herself out of such a predicament. That the bag might be found with her possessions intact was such a slim chance that it didn't warrant dwelling on. She had to reconcile herself to the fact that apart from the few dollars stuffed into the pockets of her shorts she was broke, and the consequences of that were terrifying. The hotel management was going to take a very dim view of her inability to pay the bill!

A groan slid past her lips, but steadfastly she refused to let any others follow it. There had to be a way out of this mess... there just had to! And once she'd had a good night's sleep then she would find it.

The sound of a car slowing to a halt alongside her caught her attention, and she glanced round, feeling herself go hot all over when she recognised the driver.

'Would you like a lift?' His voice was just as gravelly as she remembered it, the deep tones holding no trace of warmth.

Stephanie smiled at the child who was peering rather anxiously over his shoulder, then shook her head, her blue eyes chilly as they met his. 'No, thank you.'

She turned her head away, ignoring the throbbing of the engine, and breathed a sigh of relief as the car pulled away. However, it was short-lived as it came to a halt a few yards away and the engine was cut. The man got out, his long legs eating up the distance as he strode back to her, his face set into lines of obvious displeasure. Stephanie glanced warily at him, then looked round, but apart from a couple who were standing with arms entwined, lost in each other, a few yards away there was no one else waiting for the bus.

'I asked if you would like a lift,' the man ground out as he came to a halt in front of her and folded his arms across his broad chest.

'And I told you quite clearly that I didn't want one. Perhaps there is something wrong with your hearing, Mr...?' She paused, one slender brow raising in mocking enquiry.

'Ford. Logan Ford. And for your information, Stephanie, my hearing is perfect.'

Hearing him say her name that way startled her so much that she stared back at him in shock. 'How do you know my name?'

He smiled tightly, shooting a glance over his shoulder at the small figure who was staring rather anxiously out of the window. 'You seem to have got yourself a fan there, honey. My daughter hasn't stopped chattering about you for the past hour. I would have needed to be deaf if I hadn't caught on to your name. Now come along.' He slid a hand under her elbow and started to lead her towards the car, but Stephanie drew back, glaring at him.

'Just hold it right there! I told you that I don't want a lift and I meant it. Frankly, I can't understand why you even bothered to stop to offer me one in the first place. I didn't think we parted on terms which would make either of us anxious to meet again!'

'You're right. I don't give a damn how you get back to your hotel, or whether you achieve it safely or not. From what I've seen of you, you can well take care of yourself. However, my daughter doesn't share my enlightened views. She saw you walking towards the bus-stop and made me turn back. Seems that she's worried that something might happen to you, being all by yourself at this time of night.'

'Well, that was a kind thought. She is obviously a very considerate little girl.' Unlike her father, she silently added, then flushed when she caught his eyes and realised that he knew exactly what she'd been thinking.

Nervously she edged around the man, not liking the way his eyes had narrowed on her flushed face, or the way his strong jaw had tightened. 'Tell Jessica thank you, will you? But I don't need a lift. I'll be fine.'

His hand shot out, stopping her from moving away, his fingers almost bruising as he held her just in front of him and stared coldly down into her face. 'I'm sure you will, but Jessica won't be convinced by such a re-assurance. And I don't intend to spend the night sitting up with her while she has more nightmares, worrying about you! Now we can either do this the easy way or we can do this the hard way, but the outcome will be the same: like it or not, Stephanie, we are giving you a lift!'

He put an insulting emphasis on her given name that stung, but suddenly Stephanie didn't feel up to arguing any more. The night had taken its toll; the loss of her bag coming on top of their previous confrontation was just too much. Tears slithered down her cheeks and she turned away, hating him to see her this way.

'What the...?' The exclamation was bitten off, his surprise evident in the way his fingers bit into her flesh. Stephanie yelped, then cried all the harder, broken sobs which echoed through the night.

'Look, if this is some sort of trick, lady, then cut it out. It won't cut any ice with me!'

There wasn't an ounce of compassion in the harsh tones, not an inch of give now that he had recovered from his surprise, and Stephanie glared up at him with tear-soaked eyes.

'It isn't a trick, but I don't expect you to believe me! For your information, Mr Ford, I've had it up to here tonight, what with you being so horrible before and then losing my bag and everything! And if I feel like crying then I shall do so, and I won't have any arrogant jerk like you telling me not to!'

'I should watch my tongue if I were you. I won't have any woman speaking to me like that!'

His anger was rising, but Stephanie was too upset to care. 'Won't you indeed? Then what are you going to do about it, Mr High and Mighty Ford—wash my mouth out with soap and water? That seems to me just about—— Ohhh!'

The breath whooshed out of her as he jerked her to him so fast that she hit his chest. Instinctively her hands clutched at his shoulders to steady herself, her fingers fastening on to the iron-hard muscles that rippled under her touch. Startled, she stared up into his face, watching the faint sardonic smile that curved his chiselled lips with a feeling of alarm and something else, some other sensation that made her knees feel like rubber and her heart skip.

'There's always more than one way to bring a person in line, honey. It doesn't always need to be...unpleasant to be effective.'

His eyes dropped deliberately to her mouth, lingering for a heartbeat in a look that she could feel, then abruptly he set her from him and took a slow step back. 'Now if you've got that out of your system, shall we go? It's late, way past time that Jessica should have been in bed.'

He stepped aside for Stephanie to precede him, opening the rear door of the car with a mocking courtesy. She slid inside, then ran a hand over her face to wipe away the tears, forcing a smile as Jessica twisted round in her seat to stare at her in concern.

'You aren't crying, are you, Stephie?' She glanced at her father, who had slid behind the wheel, her mouth drooping. 'Daddy didn't shout at you, did he?'

Stephanie's eyes caught Logan's in the mirror for a long second before she looked away with a tiny sigh. How she ached to pay him back for what he'd just done, but it would be unfair to use his daughter this way. 'No... no, of course not. It wasn't his fault. I was a bit upset anyway because I'd lost my bag.'

'Your bag?' The girl's eyes rounded, then she gasped. 'I remember, you put it down on the floor when you stopped to help me. You gave me a tissue to wipe my face. Is that how you lost it?'

There was no doubting the child's concern or the faint shadow of guilt that showed on her young face. It bothered Stephanie in ways she couldn't explain. Jessica was far too young to feel guilty about something that hadn't really been her fault. 'Probably, but it was my fault. I shouldn't have been so careless. Don't you go worrying about it, love.'

'Which hotel are you staying at?' The deep voice cut into the conversation, and Stephanie forced herself to glance at the man behind the wheel, feeling the betraying colour stealing into her cheeks. That was the trouble with having such pale, fine skin: whenever she was embarrassed it showed, and she felt embarrassed now as she remembered that strange rush of weakness she'd felt when he'd held her. She must have been even more upset by everything that had gone on than she'd realised.

Hurriedly she told him the name of her hotel, then sat quietly as he drove the powerful car the short distance to pull up in the driveway. She ran a hand over her hair, smoothing the long, silky strands back into the knot on top of her head, then smiled at a point just above his right shoulder. 'Well, thank you, Mr Ford. It was...was kind of you to stop like that.'

She stumbled over the words and saw him smile with faint derision as he turned to look back at her, but there was no trace of anything in his voice apart from polite dismissal as he said levelly, 'Don't mention it.'

Obviously he was just as anxious as her to get this over and done with now that he had laid his daughter's fears to rest. Stephanie fumbled with the lock on the car door in her haste to get out, not realising that Logan Ford had got out first until the door swung smoothly open and a large, tanned hand fitted itself beneath her elbow with a murmured, 'Allow me.'

It should have been nothing more than a small courtesy to help her out, but as Stephanie slid out of the seat she made the mistake of glancing up into his face, and went cold at what she saw there. Did he view all women this way—as commodities rather than as human beings? Or was she being specially selected to bear the brunt of that assessing look that seemed to take stock of every slender line of her body with a disturbing thoroughness?

She straightened abruptly, smoothing the thin cotton shorts down her long, slim legs, wondering why she should care one way or the other what Logan Ford's views on women were. She searched his face, but it was impossible to read much from his expression as he half turned away from the dim light spilling from the hotel foyer. It was too dark to see what lay in his eyes, too dark even to bring the vibrancy of that deep red hair to life. It just showed her the outline of the man, not the substance, and with a sudden flash of insight she realised that was how he preferred it. Logan Ford was a man who would guard his thoughts and feelings, a man who would stand alone in a crowd.

'If there's nothing else I can do, then it's time we said goodnight again.'

The deep voice stopped her musings and she started self-consciously, hoping that he hadn't realised where her thoughts had been wandering. Quickly she turned and bent down to the car window, running a gentle finger down Jessica's soft little cheek as she smiled into the child's tired eyes. 'It was nice of you to stop for me. Thank you. I hope you'll have a lovely time for the rest of your stay here.'

'But what about you, Stephie? What are you going to do without your bag and things?'

Stephanie forced another smile, although that very thought was gnawing at the back of her mind. 'Don't you worry about me. I'll be fine. Now goodnight.'

She stood up and held her hand out to the tall man, forcing a cool little smile to her mouth that didn't quite match the wariness in her blue eyes. 'Thank you, Mr Ford. It was kind of you to bring me back.'

'But you would have much preferred it if I hadn't bothered?' He took her hand and held it, his fingers hard against hers.

'I never said that.'

'You didn't have to.' He studied her face for a long moment, then let her hand go. 'Don't ever be tempted to play poker, will you, Stephanie? Your face is far too expressive.'

He strode round the car and slid behind the wheel, starting the engine and driving off almost before she'd had chance to wonder what he'd meant by that cryptic comment. She sighed roughly and turned towards the beckoning lights of the hotel. What did it matter anyway? That was the last she would see of Logan Ford, and she couldn't say that she was sorry. There was something about the man that spelled out trouble, and she had quite enough of that to contend with right now. And *that* was what she had to concentrate on.

It made good sense, yet strangely, when she finally got to bed and fell into a restless sleep, it wasn't the precariousness of her situation that haunted her dreams, but the memory of a tall man with red hair and eyes the colour of the richest chocolate. Logan Ford, a true enigma; a man with a child who seemed more alone than anyone she'd ever met before.

Six dollars, twenty cents.

Stephanie stared at the neat pile of money, then picked up the bills to re-count them, praying that she'd made a mistake and mixed a twenty in with the rest. American money was extremely confusing, the different denominations of notes looking remarkably similar. However, not even a second nor a third count made a scrap of difference to the total, and her heart sank.

This was all that stood between her and destitution, this meagre sum of money which would barely pay for breakfast, let alone the cost of her stay in the hotel and a ticket home to England. What on earth was she going to do?

A knock on the door roused her from her brooding and she stood up with a sigh, smoothing a hand down over the fuchsia and white patterned shorts which she was wearing with a sleeveless white vest top. She hurried across the room to answer it, then stood frozen in shock as she recognised the man waiting outside the door. He smiled slowly, his eyes running deliberately over her figure in the revealing outfit before returning to her face with a hint of challenge in their depths.

'Aren't you going to invite me in, Stephanie?'

The husky roughness of his voice made a sudden unwanted shiver race down her spine, and she drew herself upright. 'What do you want?'

He smiled again, one brow arching with mockery. 'My, my, what a welcome, honey. Anyone would think you aren't pleased to see me.'

'I'm not,' she replied baldly, tightening her grip on the edge of the door. 'Now would you mind telling me what you want by coming here?' She glanced past him along the empty hallway. 'Where's Jessica? Haven't you brought her with you?'

'No.' With an ease which was galling, he removed her hand from the door and walked inside the room.

'Now just a minute! What do you think you're doing?' There was a trace of fear in her voice, and he turned to stare calmly back at her.

'Not what you evidently imagine I'm planning on.' He closed the door, then leant back against it while he studied her. He was dressed in a navy T-shirt this morning with white trousers which emphasised the slimness of his hips and the length of his powerful legs, and in the light pouring in through the window his hair gleamed with an unrestrained fire. He was a startlingly attractive man with that unusual colouring, the sort who would draw any woman's eyes, and Stephanie wasn't immune to his appeal.

Nervously she turned away to pick up some of the coins from the pile on the table, tossing them from hand to hand as she tried to think of something to say to dispel the mounting tension, but typically it was Logan Ford who spoke first.

'Let me make this clear from the outset: I am not here for any personal reasons. You don't need to worry that I have designs on your...virtue. This is strictly business.'

She flushed at the note in his voice which implied that she'd probably lost her claims to virtue years before. She'd had her share of admirers, her attractive looks and vivacious personality being enough to guarantee that, but she'd never felt any desire to allow the friendships to develop into intimacy. One day she would meet the man she would want to share such a relationship with, but until that happened she wouldn't settle for second best. She remembered the heartache her friend Laura had gone through when such a relationship had gone sour, and used it as a warning. She was probably far more 'virtuous' than Logan could begin to imagine, but there was no way she was going to inform him of that fact!

She returned his ironic look as levelly as she could, yet couldn't quite keep the bite from her voice. 'Then I suggest that you tell me exactly why you have come. I cannot imagine what sort of business we have with one another, Mr Ford.'

He laughed as he went and sat down on the chair, crossing one long leg over the other as he looked up at where she stood stiffly by the table. 'Did that hit a bit too close to home, Stephanie? Sorry. I merely meant to reassure you as to my intentions.'

She ignored the taunt, setting the coins down with a clatter. 'Then why are you here? If this is some sort of a game, then let me tell you that I am in no mood to play it.'

'I'm sure you're not.' He flicked a lean hand at the small pile of money. 'That's why I'm here.'

Stephanie frowned as she glanced down at the table. 'I don't understand.'

He sighed as he ran a hand through his hair to push it back from his forehead. 'It's quite simple. You told me last night that you had lost your bag, and I assume that you lost most of your money with it. Am I right?'

'Yes, but I don't see how it's any concern of yours. Look, if you feel responsible because I lost it when I was looking after Jessica, then don't.'

'Don't worry. I have no doubt it was the result of your own carelessness—that plus poking your pretty little nose in where it wasn't wanted.' He ignored her gasp of outrage as he stood up and walked over to the window, staring out for a few seconds before he turned back to her. 'However, unfortunately Jessica once again doesn't share my view. She feels that what happened was her fault, and the last thing I want right now is for her to start worrying about it.'

'I can understand that, but I explained last night that it was just an accident. I don't want her worrying about it any more than I want you to. I am quite capable of looking after myself!'

'Even in view of the fact that that is all the money you have left in your possession?' He picked up the notes and fanned them between his fingers. He had beautiful hands, long-fingered and strong, the skin deeply tanned and sprinkled with the same dark gold hair that covered his forearms. Stephanie found herself studying them, then quickly took the money from him and laid it back on the table in a gesture of defiance.

'I don't see that it is any business of yours how much money I have. Now if you have reassured yourself that I don't hold either you or Jessica to blame, may I suggest you leave? I have a lot to do, as I am sure you can appreciate.'

She turned towards the door, but he continued as though she hadn't spoken. 'As I was just saying, I don't want Jessica worrying. She's been through a lot recently without having this on her mind as well.'

The harsh note in his voice brought her head round, and she saw a flicker of regret kindle briefly in his dark eyes. It made her hesitate, when what she had been intending was to order him to leave. 'I don't understand. Has she been ill?'

He shook his head, his expression guarded once more. 'No. Her mother died recently, and naturally she's been very upset.'

'Oh, how awful for her! Poor little thing.' She flushed and added hurriedly, 'And awful for you too, of course. I am sorry, Mr Ford.'

He smiled with a faint derision. 'You can save your commiserations. Jessica's mother and I parted several years ago. Anything we may have felt for each other was gone well before she died.'

He sounded so devoid of emotion that Stephanie was shocked. 'Why, that's heartless! She was the mother of your child, after all. That should count for something, surely!'

'My relationship with Amanda isn't under discussion here. It's Jessica's well-being which concerns me.' He sounded so aloof that a shiver raced down Stephanie's body, sliding coldly along every vein. He must have cared for the woman at one time if they'd conceived a child together. Yet there had been no reflection of it in his voice, no trace of regret that the woman was dead. Was Logan Ford really as unfeeling as he appeared to be, or was it just a cover to hide emotions that ran so deep that he was afraid to admit to them?

It might have been a desire to find out which or a feeling of compassion for Jessica which made her carry on with the unsettling conversation; Stephanie didn't really know. 'Why are you telling me all this? Why have you come?'

He seemed to hesitate, studying her in silence. 'Because I believe that we can help one another. What exactly did you lose last night?'

Stephanie sighed, not understanding what he wanted with her, yet prepared to go along with him a while longer. 'Money, obviously, plus my passport, credit cards, bank cards... all those things. They were all in my bag.'

'So what do you intend to do now?'

'I was just trying to work that out when you arrived.' She sank down on the chair, worry shadowing her face. 'I can probably get an emergency passport issued via the Consul, but that's the least of my worries when I don't have the money now to pay for a ticket home.'

'Your credit card company can cover that. They should issue you with another card within a couple of days.'

'I'm sure they will, but, seeing as I have reached my credit limit, it won't help. And I doubt if they will be keen to extend it, in view of the fact that I don't have a job at present.'

'How about friends, family? Can they wire you some money? The Consul can arrange that too.'

Stephanie rubbed her aching temples as she went back over ground she'd covered time and again since she'd got up. 'I don't have family. My mother died when I was a child, and my father a few years ago. There's a cousin in London and another in Manchester, but...' She trailed off with a defeated sigh. 'The two close friends I went away with are in no better position financially than I am, even allowing for the fact that Rachel has quite enough to worry about at present and that Laura is still in Spain.' She glanced at Logan in near despair. 'There's no one I feel I can turn to for help!'

'Apart from me.' He smiled coolly when he saw the shock on her face, leaning against the edge of the table as he watched her.

'You? But why should you give me money?'

'Not give, Stephanie. Pay. I am willing to let you earn what you need to pay your bill here and to buy a ticket home.'

'Earn? But how? By doing what?' The words were barely out of her mouth when a sudden thought struck her and she shot to her feet. 'Now look here, if you mean what I think you——'

He straightened to stare down at her, big and arrogant-looking as his eyes met hers with such coldness that she felt a sudden chill. 'I doubt it. If I were you I would keep that very active imagination under control. My offer is quite straightforward; in return for agreeing to look after Jessica for the next five weeks until she goes back to school, I shall meet your expenses and provide you with board and lodging.'

'I...I don't know what to say. Why me? You don't know anything about me!'

'You'd be surprised at what I do know, Stephanie.' He stared calmly back at her. 'Stephanie Anne Jacobs, aged twenty-five, born in Manchester, occupation, when not travelling, schoolteacher.'

'How did you find that out?' There was no hiding her surprise, and she saw him smile with a faint cynicism.

'It isn't difficult with the right connections—and enough money, of course. However, none of that would make a scrap of difference to me if it weren't for the fact that Jessica seems to have taken an immediate liking to you. It was "Stephanie this" and "Stephanie that" all last night, and again this morning. She's been through a lot in the past few months, more than any child her age should have to cope with. She's also very worried that you will suffer because of her, with losing your bag. This will solve everyone's problems. All I need now is your answer—yes or no?'

'But you can't expect me to give it to you here and now.'

He smiled meaningfully, then felt in the pocket of his trousers, pulled out a thin sheet of paper, and laid it down on the table beside the money. 'I appreciate that you must want to know more about me, in view of the fact that you'll be staying in my house. I've written out a list of people who will provide references for me. Feel free to call any or all of them to check.' He glanced at the heavy watch strapped to his broad wrist, then walked smoothly to the door.

'Wait a moment! Is that it?' She hurried after him, stopping just a few feet away.

'I don't think there's anything left to say. I've told you what I'm prepared to offer you, and explained what you would be expected to do. Now it's up to you. I shall expect to hear your decision by five o'clock this afternoon. The details of my hotel are on that paper.'

He opened the door, but she stopped him with a slim hand on his arm. 'Why are you doing this for me?'

He shook his head, his face devoid of all expression. 'I am not doing it for you. Jessica needs someone to take care of her through the holidays while I'm busy at work. I had someone lined up for the job, but unfortunately it fell through, leaving me with the problem of finding a replacement at short notice. She likes you and you seem well qualified for the position. There is nothing personal about my offer, so don't make the mistake of thinking that there is.' He smiled slowly, with a contempt that made her ache for some strange reason. 'I would be the first to admit that women have their uses, but rest assured that your role will be purely that of caring for my daughter.'

Her hand slid from his arm and she stepped back, trying to control the shudder that ran through her at such a cynical assertion. What a strangely disturbing man he was, fire on the outside and ice straight through to the core!

She closed the door as he left and leant back against it as she caught her breath, but it was hard to shake off the disturbing sensations he'd left behind. She closed her eyes, hearing again the harshness in his voice as he'd spoken about Jessica's mother, and she felt a sudden surge of compassion for the dead woman.

To give one's heart to a man like Logan Ford would be an incredible act of folly that no woman should ever commit.

CHAPTER THREE

THE day crawled past until the hands on Stephanie's watch touched four, and then the minutes flew.

For the hundredth time she picked up the phone to call Logan Ford and tell him that she couldn't accept his offer than found herself putting it down again without making the call. The whole idea was crazy, totally unacceptable, so why did she find it so difficult to tell him that?

She got up and walked over to the window, watching the other guests splashing in the pool, hearing the faint sounds of their laughter carrying on the hot afternoon air. They were all enjoying themselves while here she was trying to find a solution to a problem that wouldn't be solved. She had to find enough money to pay her bill here and buy her ticket back home to England, but how? Apart from Logan there was just no one she could turn to!

The loud knock at the door brought her spinning round and she hurried across the room, half expecting to find the tall red-haired man outside the door, but it wasn't him.

'Miss Jacobs?' At her nod of agreement the man continued, a trace of discomfort on his face as he held an envelope out to her. 'The manager has asked me to give you this, ma'am.'

'What is it?' She took it from him, studying the unmarked white envelope in confusion.

'Your bill. It's made up until today and we shall be grateful if you could arrange to pay it as soon as possible.'

'My bill? But I'm not due to leave until the day after tomorrow. What is this all about?'

The man ran a finger round the collar of his spotless white shirt, his discomfort even more in evidence now. 'I'm afraid there seems to have been a mix-up in the bookings. We shall have to ask you to vacate this room tomorrow by ten a.m. at the latest. I'm very sorry.'

'So am I!' She glared at the man, but he had already turned to hurry along the corridor. Stephanie closed the door then ripped the envelope open, staring down at the neatly totalled account with panic in her eyes. Now what was she going to do? She could only speculate on what had happened to alert the hotel management to her possible inability to pay, and in a way she could sympathise with their dilemma, but it didn't help her situation one little bit! Between now and ten a.m. tomorrow she had to come up with just over two hundred dollars or suffer the consequences!

When the telephone suddenly rang she snatched it up, a trace of panic echoing in her voice. 'Yes? Hello?'

'Is there something wrong?'

She recognised the voice immediately, felt the roughness of its deep timbre rolling along every taut nerve. Deliberately she took a long, slow breath, trying to stave off her first impulse to throw herself on his mercy and beg for help—unconditional help, that was. Logan Ford wasn't the sort of man who would be affected by any pleas for help.

'You could say that. The manager of the hotel has just presented me with a bill for my stay, and informed me that unfortunately there has been a mix-up and that my room will have to be vacated by ten tomorrow morning.'

'I see. That could pose rather a problem, couldn't it? What do you intend to do?' His voice was completely bland, so why did she have the sudden horrible suspicion that he knew rather more about what had happened than he was admitting to? Anger rose inside her and she pressed the receiver tightly to her ear, wishing that he were in the room so that she could see his face.

'I don't suppose you have any idea why they should have become worried that I might not be able to pay?'

'Should I?'

'That isn't an answer! Look, Mr Ford, if you were behind this, then let me tell you that I——'

He cut her off, his voice hard and determined. 'Let's not make a song and dance out of this, Miss Jacobs. Does it really matter when they presented you with the bill? The situation would still be the same; you can't pay it, can you?'

All the fight went out of her as quickly as it had arisen, and she sank down on the edge of the chair. 'No. You know I can't.'

'Then what do you propose to do about it? Have you made your decision about whether you intend to take up my offer?'

'I...' She swallowed hard to ease the knot of tension in her throat, wondering what to say. It seemed like the only way out of this mess, yet something made her hesitate about accepting his proposal. She searched her mind, trying to work out what it was that bothered her most, but could come up with nothing but a vague feeling that she might be courting even worse trouble than what she was already in. Logan Ford was a disturbing man; he disturbed her in ways that she didn't want to think about. But there again, he'd assured her that it was his daughter she would be dealing with, not him. Was she simply being stupid to refuse this lifeline?

'Well? I haven't got all day to waste, Stephanie.' There was rough impatience in his voice, and she started nervously, snapping back at him. 'It isn't that easy! Can't you understand that?'

'Frankly, no. I have made you a very generous offer. I can't see what is so difficult about making up your mind what you intend to do.'

'Why can't you just lend me the money? I would pay you back; you have my word on that!'

He laughed softly, a low sound that made a *frisson* work down her spine, like a finger smoothing her skin. 'I'm sure you would; however, I'm not in the business of making loans. You know what I'm offering, but if it isn't acceptable to you then we had better call the whole deal off. Good luck, Stephanie; I think you're going to need it.'

The line went dead. Stephanie stared at the receiver in shock, then slowly replaced it, gnawing on her lower lip. He hadn't even given her a chance to explain her concerns! He was so damned ruthless that he couldn't spare the time to listen. But now what was she going to do?

She sat worrying over it until the pangs of hunger growing in her stomach drove her from her room. She took the lift down and fed two of her precious dollar bills into the machine in the back hallway, grimacing as it disgorged a frosted can of drink and a packaged Danish pastry. It was a meagre meal, but the best she could do.

'Beggars can't be choosers' was an old adage that was being proved very true.

She carried the food out to the terrace that overlooked the pool and sat down at one of the tables, leaning back against the hard metal chair with a weary sigh that echoed into the night. Peeling the wrapper off the pastry, she took a bite then had to force herself to chew the sticky confection. It seemed to lodge itself in her throat, held there by the huge knot of panic and tension. Popping the tab on the can, she took a long swallow of the icy liquid, then set the can down with a clatter. Who was she kidding? She knew exactly what she needed to do to get herself out of this mess, and she was just being stupid by not admitting it. It would probably stick in her throat even more than the pastry, but she was going to have to go to Logan Ford and hope that he would cut her a very large slice of humble pie.

The worse thing was the wretched man would probably enjoy watching her eat it!

The hotel lobby was bustling when she walked through the door. Stephanie waited her turn at the reception desk, then asked the girl behind the counter to ring through to Mr Ford's room and tell him that she would like to speak to him.

'I'm afraid that Mr Ford has just left for the evening, ma'am. Would you like to leave a message? I can see that he gets it as soon as he... Wait a minute; isn't that him over there? He must have come back to get something.'

Stephanie's heart had sunk at the news that he was out, and now it leapt back to life, beating painfully fast as she looked across to where the receptionist was pointing. Her eyes met his in one long look, and she felt her temper rise. He'd known she would come! Somehow, some way, he'd been expecting her, and the thought was galling!

She sucked in a deep breath, trying desperately to hang on to her temper, but when a voice spoke in her ear she swung round and glared at the tall man standing by her side.

'Changed your mind, Stephanie?'

'You know damned well that I have! I didn't have any option, did I?'

Her voice had risen, and several people in the queue glanced curiously at them. Logan took her arm, his grasp harsh and uncompromising as he led her away from the desk into a secluded corner where they wouldn't be overheard. 'I don't like scenes, understand? Whatever business we have has nothing to do with anyone but us. So keep your voice down if you hope to have me repeat the offer you so recently turned down.'

She would have given anything in the whole wide world to be able to tell him what he could do with his offer, but both of them knew she wasn't in any position to do that. 'If there were any other way that I could get the money I need, Mr Ford...'

'You wouldn't be here. And if I didn't need someone to look after Jessica so desperately, then I would never have asked you. So I imagine that makes us even. Now all I need to know is when we can collect you tomorrow.'

'Tomorrow? Oh, but I didn't expect that you would need me immediately! I imagined that you would want to finish your holiday first.' There was no disguising her shock, and he smiled slowly, his dark eyes boring into her.

'Jessica and I shall be returning home tomorrow morning. We've already spent the best part of a week here in Orlando and, frankly, I can't spare any more time. What did you expect to happen, Stephanie? That I would pay your hotel bill and meet your expenses for the next few days without your having to do anything in return?'

She flushed. 'No! I never expected that at all. I am willing to earn every penny, Mr Ford. I don't want charity, especially not from you!'

His mouth thinned with displeasure as he took a step towards her. 'Don't you think your attitude is rather foolish, seeing as you are dependent on me for so much? I appreciate that you must find this situation you're in galling in the extreme, but you must admit that you have been extremely fortunate. If I hadn't made you this offer, then just imagine what might have happened.'

She could! She'd spent best part of the day going over the possibilities in her head, hour after hour. Finding herself broke and stranded in a foreign country was like a nightmare! She swallowed her pride, forcing the anger from her voice as she replied quietly, 'I apologise. I suppose I must sound ungrateful. I do——'

'Stephie!' The delight in the child's voice was apparent as she hurried across the foyer towards them. Stephanie turned towards the girl with a sigh of relief, only too glad of the interruption. What was it about Logan Ford that aroused her anger so easily? She wished she knew, because it was going to be an uncomfortable few weeks if she jumped every time he spoke. Somehow she was going to have to learn to ignore the effect he had on her, but it wouldn't be easy. Logan Ford wasn't the kind of man one could ignore!

'Hello, Jessica. How are you?'

'Fine, but what are you doing here? Daddy didn't tell me that you were coming.' There was curiosity on the child's pale face, a sparkle of interest in her eyes, and Stephanie smiled warmly at her.

'Maybe that's because he didn't know I was coming.' She glanced up at Logan, watching the way his eyes narrowed at the barely veiled sarcasm in her voice. She sighed softly, realising that she was doing it again, declaring warfare when she was in no position to fight the battle.

'Did you, Daddy?' Jessica caught Logan's hand, drawing his attention back to her. He smiled at once, his face softening as he looked down at his daughter. Stephanie felt her heart beat a shade or two faster at the unexpected tenderness she could see on his face. When he looked like that, his chiselled lips curled into a genuine smile, his eyes warm, he was devastatingly attractive, and everything female in her responded in a way that shocked her.

'Did I what?' he asked with mock-solemnity as he teased the child.

'Know that Stephie was coming, of course!' Jessica sighed noisily, letting go of his hand to stare up at him. 'You know what I mean!'

'Mmm. Let me just say that I had a good idea she might come, even if I wasn't one hundred per cent certain.' There was open derision on his face as he glanced over his daughter's head, and Stephanie felt herself go cold as she realised that he had quite deliberately evened the score between them. Abruptly she turned away to stare across the empty foyer, wondering why she felt so hurt. This man meant nothing to her;

he was a stranger who had offered her help more for his own reasons than hers. It shouldn't have mattered what he thought about her, but she was honest enough to admit that it did.

Suddenly she couldn't take any more of this verbal fencing. She turned to smile at Jessica, studiously avoiding Logan's eyes. 'You were about to go out when I arrived, and I don't want to spoil your evening. Your father can explain everything to you, Jessica.'

'Oh, but you can't go yet! Can she, Daddy?' Jessica's voice held a note of pleading as she appealed to her father.

'Of course not. Quite apart from anything else, Stephanie, there are a few things we need to discuss. If you haven't had dinner yet, then perhaps you will join us?'

Dinner? On six dollars? He must know that she hadn't, but she refused to give him the satisfaction of hearing her admit it. 'I've already eaten, thank you.' It was a lie, but such a small one, and she salved her noisy conscience with thoughts of the pastry.

'Then I'm sure you won't mind sitting with us while we eat.' He took Stephanie's arm, leading her out of the hotel and putting her into the car before she had time to frame any further objections. Jessica scrambled into the back seat, chattering excitedly, blissfully unaware of the tension. Stephanie waited until Logan started the car and Jessica was engaged in playing with a doll she'd plucked from the door pocket before letting him know exactly what she thought of his high-handedness.

'I said that I didn't want to come with you. Just who do you think you are, commandeering me like this?'

He barely spared her a glance, his eyes focused on the traffic as they joined the expressway. 'I am the man who is employing you now. I am paying good money for your company, and I intend to see that I get full value. If I want you to come with us, then you will come; otherwise we may as well terminate our agreement right now.'

'You may be employing me to look after your daughter, but that doesn't mean that you own me!' Anger lent a fire to her blue eyes, added a tinge of colour to her cheeks, and she saw him smile as he glanced round at her.

'What exactly is bothering you most, Stephanie? The fact that you can't see another way out of this mess you're in, or that I'm the one calling all the shots?'

'I don't know what you mean!' She drew back against the door, suddenly wary of what he meant and the way he was watching her.

He shrugged lightly, his shoulder brushing hers, sending an instant surge of sensation flowing through her body. She caught her breath, fighting the strange feeling of weakness the light touch evoked, but there was no way she could control the shudder that ran through her when he answered in that deep, harsh voice, 'Don't you? I think you do, and that is why you are so angry. Would you prefer our relationship to have been based on different terms, rather than that of employer and employee?'

'I... Why, that's ridiculous!' Colour swam up her cheeks as she stared at him in horror.

'Why is it ridiculous? You spilled that drink over me yesterday, obviously for a reason. Why should it be so ridiculous to assume that you would prefer to be on more intimate terms with me than an employee would enjoy?'

'It was an accident! Someone jogged my arm. I didn't do it deliberately to...to...' Her throat closed on the allegation, but he didn't seem to suffer from her nervousness.

'Pick me up? Is that what you're finding so hard to say? Don't be shy, Stephanie. This is an enlightened era. If a woman sees a man she wants, then there is no reason for her not to be the one to make the first approach.' He turned the car into the car park of a brightly lit steak bar, cutting the engine. Jessica scrambled from the back and ran across to look at the fish swimming in the huge ornamental pool in the forecourt, leaving Stephanie and Logan suddenly alone. He leant towards her, his eyes holding hers in the dim light from the dashboard, his tone dropping to a note of intimacy that made her nerves tingle.

'I noticed you watching me yesterday, Stephanie. *Before* you spilled that drink all over me. I'm not a vain man, but it isn't the first time that a woman has made her interest known. Don't be shy about admitting to it now. It's better that we clear the air, once and for all.'

She couldn't help the guilty blush that ran up her throat. She *had* been watching him yesterday, mesmerised by his whole appearance and that aura of power that surrounded him. He laughed deeply, catching her chin when she tried to turn her head away to avoid his knowing gaze. Tilting her face up to his, he stared her straight in the eyes. 'I said yesterday that your face was almost too expressive, so don't bother lying, honey. It isn't worth the effort. All I want is to get things straight before we go any further. You are an attractive woman, Stephanie, extremely attractive, but I doubt if you need me to tell you that. I learned a long time ago that most women are very aware of the power they can wield over a man.'

There was cool contempt on his face as he studied her, and she shifted uncomfortably, trying to break the light hold he had on her chin, but he wasn't ready to let her go, it seemed.

She forced herself to meet those hard, dark eyes, refusing to let him see how disturbed she felt. 'What do you expect me to say, Mr Ford? Thank you for the compliment?' She arched a brow, then wished she'd held her tongue when his mouth thinned.

'I wasn't trying to pay you compliments, Stephanie. I was merely stating a fact. You are an attractive woman who is obviously well aware of the fact. I doubt you would have survived your recent trip if you hadn't been. However, I never make the mistake of mixing business with pleasure. Understand? I am employing you solely to care for Jessica. If you have any ideas about adding extra duties to your workload, then I suggest that you forget them. It will save both of us a great deal of embarrassment, I imagine.'

He didn't have the first idea what the word embarrassment meant, but she did! She had never felt so embarrassed or so annoyed in the whole of her life! 'Now look here, Logan Ford, I don't care who you are or how many eager willing women have thrown themselves at you in the past, but you can think again if you imagine that I'm one of them! To phrase it in terms you should have no difficulty in understanding: I am *not* interested. You leave me cold!'

'Is that a fact?' With a speed that shocked her, he drew her to him, holding her so close that she could feel the heavy beat of his heart against her breast. Slowly he lifted his hand and ran a fingertip down her cheek, letting it stop just a fraction from the corner of her mouth as he stared into her widened eyes. Stephanie held her breath, almost afraid to breathe, terrified of doing anything that would cause another reaction, but it was impossible to quell the tiny shudder that rippled helplessly through her as he let his fingertip move again to skate lightly, shockingly, across her mouth.

He laughed softly, a faint rumble of sound that filled the air with tension, and she flinched nervously. 'So I leave you cold, do I, honey?'

'Yes.' She wanted to shout the word back into his arrogant face, to throw the allegation back at him with scorn, but her voice was just a touch too breathless to be convincing.

He set her from him just as suddenly as he'd caught hold of her, his face cold and unyielding. 'We both know that's a lie, now more than ever. So remember what I said, Stephanie, and don't let yourself imagine that I might be tempted by your undoubted charms. I am employing you to do a job; just stick to that and we shall get along fine.'

He thrust the car door open, not bothering to wait for her as he joined Jessica beside the pool. Stephanie counted to ten, slowly, but it didn't seem to help one bit. He was the most impossible, arrogant man she'd ever met, and if it weren't for the fact that she needed his money she would have got straight out of this car and walked away! When she thought about having to spend the next few weeks in his company... Well!

She climbed out of the car and slammed the door, glaring at his broad back. It might be ungrateful, but somehow, some way, she was going to find a way to make him regret he'd ever said that to her, because it was about time that Mr Logan 'Arrogant' Ford was taught a lesson he would never forget!

CHAPTER FOUR

THE car arrived to collect Stephanie a little after eight the next morning. She had already brought her case down, and was waiting outside when it turned into the driveway. When Logan had driven her back the previous night he had settled her account at the desk, and she hadn't wanted to go through a rerun of that experience. Remembering it now, she felt her face go hot with colour, and she hurriedly bent down to gather her things together, trying to push the thoughts to the back of her mind, but it would be a long time before she forgot that look of speculation on the manager's face when Logan had paid her bill!

'Give me that.' He brushed her hand aside, lifting the heavy suitcase from her grasp with an ease that was galling, to carry it over to the car and slide it into the boot. He glanced back at her, impatience showing briefly on his handsome face as she made no move. 'Well, what are you waiting for? You do have everything, I assume?'

What was she waiting for? The cavalry to come and rescue her, or the police to arrive with her missing bag, offering her a last-minute reprieve? Stephanie glanced round the quiet gardens of the hotel, breathing in the warm, sweet air like a person condemned, wishing there was some way she could stop this from happening, but nothing came to mind. Logan had paid her bill, would buy her ticket, and in exchange acquire her services for the next five long weeks. How would she survive?

'For heaven's sake, woman!' With a muttered oath he walked back to where she was standing and took her arm, almost dragging her towards the car in his impatience.

Stephanie dragged her arm away, rubbing her tingling flesh as she glared at him. 'Do you mind? I don't like being manhandled.'

'Then I suggest that you get a move on. I haven't got all day to waste. I have a business meeting later on this afternoon that can't be put off because you're having second thoughts!'

'If I am having second thoughts, then is it any wonder? You have a real attitude problem, Mr Ford. Has nobody told you that before?'

He wrenched the car door open, his eyes like black ice as they skimmed her face. 'I find that people usually have more sense than to say things like that to me, Stephanie.'

There was a touch of menace in the gravelly voice, and she felt a momentary reluctance to goad him any further, but that demon that always seemed to surface when he was around pushed her on. 'Is that so? Why? Because they are afraid of you. Well, you don't scare me, mister! I shall say exactly what I think when I think it... understand?'

His brows drew together, his expression thunderous, and she felt her heart skip a beat as it occurred to her that she might just have pushed him that bit too far. Then suddenly he laughed, a hint of admiration on his face as he held the door wide. 'It makes a change to have someone stand up to me, Stephanie, if you want the truth. That's the trouble with money and power: the more you get of both, the less people tell you what they

'Yes, she used the child...any time she felt she wanted to hit out at me, which was often. Amanda was a spoilt and petulant woman, who cared about herself more than anyone. She would use Jessica any way she could if the mood took her, refusing to let me see her when I visited. However, I soon put a stop to that once I realised what her game was.' He opened the car door, then glanced back at Stephanie's shocked face. 'So don't ever make the mistake of trying that, will you, honey? Otherwise you'll regret ever accepting this offer I made.'

He got out of the car, waiting while Stephanie joined him, his face betraying little now of the emotion she'd just witnessed. How her heart ached to say something to ease the anger he felt, but what could she say? He wouldn't welcome her interfering in something that was in truth not her concern, and the thought hurt in a way that it shouldn't have done. She was his employee now, nothing more; it shouldn't matter to her how he felt. Last night she'd wanted to do no more than teach him a lesson for being so arrogant, and she had to remember that and cling to those feelings. She couldn't afford to let herself see Logan Ford in any other light.

'Jessica is in the pool. We'd better go and get her.'

'Surely you didn't leave her there by herself?' There was no way she could disguise the immediate concern she felt, and she saw him stiffen.

'No, I didn't leave her by herself. I am quite capable of taking care of my daughter without guidance from you or anyone. She's playing with another child she's made friends with, and the mother offered to watch over both of them while I went to collect you.'

Stephanie was suitably rebuked and said nothing further as they walked round to the rear of the hotel and made their way through the extensive gardens to the huge pool with its surrounding sun-beds. There were few people in the water and even fewer lying on the padded loungers at this time of the day, so she had no difficulty in picking Jessica out. She was sitting cross-legged on one of the loungers, playing with another little girl, but as soon as she spotted her father and Stephanie she came rushing to them.

'You did come, Stephie!'

Stephanie smiled at the eager note in the child's voice, bending down to give her a quick hug before drawing back to grimace at the wet patch that had formed on the front of her blouse from Jessica's damp swimsuit. 'Of course I came. Mind you, I don't know if I should have hugged you. Look at my blouse, you little horror.'

The child's face closed up, her huge eyes brimming with sudden tears as she stared at the wet stain. 'I'm sorry. Really sorry!'

Shocked by such a reaction to her teasing, Stephanie dropped to her knees and tilted the child's face to look her straight in the eye. 'I was just joking, Jessica. Teasing you. It really doesn't matter. The blouse will dry in minutes in this heat.'

'Are you sure? Mummy used to get very cross if I messed up her clothes.' There was still a hint of uncertainty in the child's voice, and Stephanie looked up at Logan for guidance, then felt herself grow cold at the fury on his face. Who was it directed at? Her? However, before she had time to work out the answer a soft feminine voice broke in on the conversation.

'Surely you haven't come to collect Jessica already, have you? I was hoping that she could play with Lauren a while longer.'

really mean. Having you around should be a refreshing change. Now if you don't mind getting into the car, it's time we collected Jessica.'

Stephanie slid into the car without another word, suddenly anxious not to pursue the conversation. She smoothed the short, pleated pale pink skirt, then fussed with the neck of the toning floral sleeveless blouse she'd teamed it up with, feeling strangely nervous as Logan slid behind the wheel. She shot him a quick glance, letting her eyes linger for a moment on his strong profile, the vibrant hair which curled almost to the collar of his pale blue sports shirt, which he was wearing with beautifully cut silver-grey trousers, and felt a shiver of apprehension unlike anything she'd ever felt before.

She could cope with this man when he was being rude and arrogant and overbearing, but how would she fare if he ever let her see the softer side of him she sensed lay hidden beneath that tough exterior? If the way her blood was thundering and her heart was hammering after that brief compliment he'd paid her was any measure of the effect he could have, then she would have to be extremely careful.

'I hope you don't intend to keep this up.'

She jumped when he spoke, watching the way his hands slid the steering-wheel smoothly and confidently around as he steered the big car into a space in front of his hotel. He would do everything like that, she thought suddenly—confidently, aware of his own power and ability. He was a self-contained man who would trust no one to make decisions or give orders except himself. He would always be in total control.

He swore softly as he caught her wrist in his powerful hand, making her suddenly aware of the fact that she hadn't answered his question. Soft colour swam into her face and she looked away, feeling the heat of his fingers burning their brand around the slender bones of her wrist. 'I... I'm sorry. I was just wool-gathering. What did you ask me?'

He let her arm go, leaning back in the seat. 'I said that I hoped you weren't going to keep up the silent treatment all day. If you have any quarrel with me, Stephanie, then let's hear it. I won't have Jessica upset just because you feel that you have some sort of a grievance against me!'

And she had fondly imagined that he had a soft side! The man was granite through and through. She tilted her head proudly, meeting his eyes. 'I am not giving you the silent treatment. And I wouldn't dream of using Jessica that way.'

'No?' He smiled coldly. 'Then you must be one of a kind, honey.'

'What do you mean?'

'That from my experience most women will use anything and everything within their grasp to get back at a man.'

She frowned, looking behind the statement to find the cause, and felt her heart turn over with sudden pain. 'You're talking about Jessica's mother, aren't you? Did she use Jessica in some way to get back at you, Logan?'

She wasn't even aware of using his first name, her attention all centred on what he would answer. Then when he did finally speak she almost wished she hadn't asked the question in the first place. There was so much anger in his deep voice, an echo of an old torment that still ran deep.

Stephanie glanced round, studying the woman who was standing so close to Logan now that her arm brushed his. She was very beautiful in a perfectly packaged, rather over-groomed way, her blonde hair arranged in fresh curls around her exquisitely made-up face, her lush curves attractively displayed under the transparent shirt she'd slipped on over a figure-hugging fuchsia swimsuit. Even as Stephanie watched, she placed a perfectly manicured hand on Logan's tanned arm, her voice taking on a girlish playfulness that somehow grated on Stephanie's nerves.

'I'm sure you don't need to rush off quite so soon, do you?'

Logan smiled easily, letting his dark eyes linger for a meaningful moment on the woman. 'I wish I didn't need to, but business is business, Mrs Cooper.'

'Oh, but that's much too formal. Call me Melissa... please. After all, I've been divorced for over a year now.'

The warm tones were coated with so much sugar that Stephanie felt a sudden surge of nausea. She stood up abruptly, drawing the woman's attention to her. Cold green eyes made a quick assessment and then, obviously reassured by what they'd seen, moved back to Logan. Stephanie could feel her temper creeping up the Richter scale, heading for an earthquake of immense proportions. Just who did that woman think she was, looking at her...? The rest of what she'd been thinking was cut off when Logan spoke, and, instead of aiming it at the woman, Stephanie found another outlet for her anger.

'I'd be honoured, Melissa, but only if you'll call me Logan.' His voice was warm honey, smooth, flowing, no hint now of the roughness that usually edged his replies to *her*! He was turning on the charm, quite deliberately, and for some reason Stephanie hated to be a witness to it. Abruptly she caught Jessica by the hand, then looked over her head at the couple, her blue eyes filled with sparks she was quite unable to hide even if she'd been aware they were there.

'I think it would be better if I helped Jessica get changed, don't you, *Mr* Ford? After all, you do have that business meeting.'

'That sounds like a good idea.' There was just the faintest trace of amusement lurking in the depths of his eyes, but Stephanie didn't wait to question the reason for it. Turning away, she headed back to the hotel, stopping reluctantly when he called her name.

'Yes?' she snapped, barely sparing him a glance.

'You'll need the key. Here you are.' He held it out to her, forcing her to walk the few steps back to take it from his hand. Hurriedly she reached for it, then jumped when his fingers closed over hers to hold her. He lowered his voice, careful not to let it carry to Melissa, who had moved a few yards away, obviously bored with the proceedings now that she had established her position. 'Don't forget why you're here, will you, Stephanie? You're looking after Jessica, nothing more. Understand? So keep any little displays of jealousy to yourself.'

Jealousy? He really thought that she was jealous of him and that woman? For a stunned moment she could barely think, let alone deny the ridiculous allegation. Then number ten on the Richter scale was reached in one quick surge. She glared back at him, then let her eyes drift to the other woman before returning to his face with contempt. 'Don't flatter yourself, Ford! It will be a cold day in hell when I'm ever jealous over you.

From what I can see, you and she are perfect for one another—two people who have a hugely inflated opinion of their own desirability!'

His eyes narrowed, his fingers biting just a shade harder around hers. 'Think so? Maybe you're right, but one thing is certain, honey, and that is that you will never have a chance to test out just how desirable I might be.'

He let her go, turning away to join the blonde woman at the poolside. He said something in a low, confiding tone, and her husky laughter carried on the warm breeze back to Stephanie. Stephanie closed her eyes, waiting for the eruption to end all eruptions to hit her, but strangely she felt no anger now, just a huge great sense of sadness, as though she'd lost something from her life...something that had never really been hers in the first place.

It was lunchtime when they arrived at the house. Stephanie had spent the journey focusing her attention on keeping Jessica occupied on the drive, but she'd still had time to marvel at the dramatic change in scenery. Not so many years ago Orlando had been just a sleepy country town surrounded by orange groves. The arrival of the Walt Disney organisation and all the subsequent tourists had changed all that. Now the city had a squeaky-clean appearance, the vast numbers of new buildings, ultra-modern in design, aimed at providing everyone with a first-rate service while they enjoyed their holidays. But as they travelled further north towards Ocala, where Logan lived, Stephanie was struck by the shift away from glittering concrete and glass to an architecture that hinted at a more gracious past, and by the greenness of the lush pastures where horses grazed under the midday sun.

'It's lovely.' She couldn't hide her genuine appreciation, and Logan smiled with a hint of warmth.

'It is. I've never regretted moving here. There seems to be so much more space, room to breathe.'

'Where did you live before?' she asked idly, smiling at the sight of a mother and foal cantering across a meadow.

'More places than I can count.' His tone indicated that he didn't want to continue the conversation, and Stephanie bit back a sigh as she turned to smile at the child in the back of the car. Why was he always on the defensive like that? Surely it wouldn't have hurt for him to tell her just a bit about himself?

'Glad that you're nearly home, Jessica?' she asked quietly.

The child nodded, glancing out of the window, her face lighting up as she saw the horses. 'Yes. Daddy said that I can have a horse soon. Can you ride, Stephie?'

'Not very well, I'm afraid.'

'Then Daddy can teach you as well as me.' The child's face clouded for a moment. 'Mummy kept promising to teach me, but she never did.'

'It's sometimes difficult to get around to doing everything you want to, poppet,' Stephanie said softly, smoothing the red curls back from Jessica's face. 'I'm sure your mummy would have taught you if she'd had time.'

Jessica nodded, turning away to watch the horses through the window. Stephanie waited until she was sure that she was engrossed, then turned to Logan.

'How long is it...?' She left the rest of the sentence unsaid, but he understood immediately. His hands clenched on the steering-wheel, his knuckles showing through the skin. Stephanie felt a sudden urge to reach out and smooth her fingers over them to ease the painful grip, but she curbed it, knowing he would take immediate offence at even the smallest gesture of comfort.

'Three months,' he replied tautly. He glanced in the rear-view mirror, his face unreadable as he studied the child.

'It isn't long. It's only natural that she should still miss her.'

'Is it?' His voice was a rough growl of sound, anger rippling through each syllable as he turned his gaze on Stephanie. 'You know that, do you?'

'Yes.' She faced him squarely, refusing to back down in the face of an anger she barely understood. 'I was just about Jessica's age when my mother died. I remember how much I missed her...still miss her at times.'

'I see. And because of that you think you understand what Jessica has been through? Is that what you're saying?' There was biting contempt in the question and she hesitated about answering, then forced herself to carry on.

'Yes. I imagine I have a pretty good idea how she feels. But obviously you don't agree with me, Mr Ford.'

'No, I don't. I doubt if you have any idea at all, because I doubt the circumstances would be at all similar. So if you think that you can apply a few neat theories to what is troubling my daughter, then I suggest you forget them. You're here to take care of her while I'm at work. I don't want you meddling in anything you don't understand.'

He swung the car off the road between two white gateposts, slowing as he drove towards the house she could see in the distance, its white paintwork glistening against the backdrop of green velvet fields. It was absolutely beautiful—both the house, with its gracious old-world charm, and the setting—a small piece of paradise that should have thrilled her with just the thought that she was going to spend the next five weeks here. But as he stopped the car at the bottom of a shallow flight of steps, Stephanie had the craziest urge to turn and beg him to take her back. She took a long shallow breath as she stared at the house, then let her eyes stray to the man at her side and felt a sudden fear engulf her. It might be crazy, but something told her that life would never be the same for her from here on in. She was about to enter Logan's home, Logan's life, and, whether he liked it or not, what had happened in his past was going to have its effect on her future as well as his.

'And this is Daddy's bedroom.' Gripping her hand hard, Jessica dragged Stephanie in through the bedroom door, unaware of the woman's marked reluctance to enter Logan's room. She ran over to the bed and sat down on the edge of it, staring back at Stephanie with wide eyes.

'Well, do you like it, Stephie?' She made a face as she stared round the austere room. 'It's not nearly as pretty as my room, is it?'

Stephanie glanced round, her eyes lingering on the heavy oak furniture, the very masculine colour scheme—a mixture of greys and blacks, barely relieved by the odd touch of white in the draped curtains. It was a man's room all right; there was no doubting that. There was no hint of any feminine touch throughout the whole room, and somehow that surprised her, because it didn't strike her that Logan was a man who didn't care for the company of women. Far from it. With those devastating looks he must have attracted them by the score, yet none of them had left her mark on his room.

'Stephie!' She started when Jessica said her name loudly, and forced a smile.

'Sorry, love, I was miles away, but you are right. Daddy's room isn't nearly as pretty as yours.'

Satisfied by the reply, Jessica leapt off the bed and dashed towards the door, eager to show Stephanie the rest of the large house. Stephanie followed more slowly, her eyes lingering thoughtfully on the stark colour scheme, the furniture that had been chosen for comfort and little else. She had the feeling that Logan had chosen everything deliberately so that there could be no doubt that he bowed to no one's taste except his own. Had Jessica's mother shared this room with him? Somehow she doubted it. It seemed unlikely that the woman would have left so little mark on the choice of furnishings. Perhaps that had been part of the trouble, one of the reasons why she and Logan had parted. It would be hard for any woman to accept that she counted for so little in a man's life.

'Getting yourself acquainted with the layout, Stephanie?'

She jumped when Logan spoke behind her, guilty colour surging into her face, as though he had caught her doing something she shouldn't. She swung round so fast that the heel of her sandal snagged in the thick pile of the grey carpet, tipping her off balance. He caught her at once, his hands quite impersonal as he set her back on her feet, but she could feel the separate mark of each of his fingers burning her skin. Quickly she drew away from him, moving further into the room as she put more space between them.

'Jessica brought me in here. She wanted to show me your room... along with all the others, of course.' Her voice sounded breathless, but she consoled herself with the thought that it was natural with the way she had nearly fallen.

He studied her flushed face in silence, then strolled into the room, walking past her to open the window wide. The breeze billowed the white lace curtains, bringing with it the scent of grass and sunshine. In the distance Stephanie could hear an engine throbbing quietly, voices murmuring, but the sounds were so much in the distance that they seemed to have no part in what was happening in this room.

'Jessica doesn't like my bedroom very much. She thinks it's very dull and boring. What do you think, Stephanie?' Logan's voice was in keeping with the mood, the deep tones softer than she'd ever heard them. It seemed to smooth across her skin then seep deep into her pores, making her whole body throb with a deeply unsettling tension. Stephanie shifted uneasily, avoiding his eyes as she looked around the room and wondered what to say.

He laughed suddenly, just as softly, just as disturbingly. Moving away from the window, he came to stand in front of her, so close that if she stretched out her hand she could have touched him. Deliberately she clenched her hands at her sides, shocked by the sudden compulsion to do such a thing. None of the easy, uncomplicated friendships she'd enjoyed with the opposite sex in the past had prepared her for this sense of awareness. Those had been a part of her girlhood, but with Logan she was suddenly achingly conscious of being a woman.

'Surely you aren't afraid to give me an honest opinion, are you, honey? I distinctly recall you stating that you would say exactly what you thought, so what's stopping you now?'

He was deliberately pushing her, using that cold mockery to elicit a reply, but why? Why did he care what she thought? Stephanie shot him a look to try to gauge his reasons, but it was impossible to read anything in those dark eyes. Annoyance raced through her, stemming as much from her own apparent vulnerability as from what he was doing, and she stared haughtily at him. 'I can't imagine why you want to hear my views, Mr Ford. I'm here to look after Jessica, as you've been at great pains to point out to me, so why should it matter what I think about your choice of furnishings?'

He smiled slowly, white teeth gleaming against the smooth tanned skin. He looked so devastatingly handsome that Stephanie felt her heart give a funny little shudder she instantly quashed. 'So it still rankles, does it, honey? The fact that I am refusing to succumb to your undoubted charms?'

'No, it doesn't rankle! Don't kid yourself that I am——'

'Excuse me. I didn't realise you had someone with you, Logan. I'll call back later.'

The unfamiliar voice broke in on the conversation, startling them both. Stephanie turned round, a faint colour stealing up her cheeks as she suddenly saw the tall dark-haired man standing in the doorway. It was obvious from the hastily controlled expression on his face just *what* he thought he was interrupting, and was it any wonder when one considered where he'd just found them and the fact that the tension in the room was so thick that it could be cut with a knife?

She turned back to Logan, willing him to make the necessary explanations and save her any further embarrassment, but he merely smiled at the tall stranger. 'Good to see you, Cade. Was there something you needed to speak to me about?'

The man ran a hand through his black hair, his green eyes hooded as they shifted fleetingly to Stephanie's flushed face. 'Nothing that can't wait. Sorry to interrupt you both, ma'am...Logan.'

He turned to go, but there was no way that Stephanie was letting him leave thinking that...that there was something going on between her and Logan Ford! She stepped forward abruptly. 'There's no need to go. Mr Ford and I have finished our discussion.' She held her hand out, forcing herself to smile coolly at the man and not show how annoyed she was at the position Logan had placed her in. 'I'm Stephanie Jacobs. Mr Ford has hired me to take care of Jessica for the next few weeks.'

The man took her hand, engulfing it in his own far larger one. 'A pleasure to meet you, Miss Jacobs. The name's Rylance, Cade Rylance. I manage Logan's stud farm. I hope you enjoy your stay here with us.'

Stephanie smiled, warmed by the open admiration in the man's beautiful green eyes. 'I'm sure I will. But you must call me Stephanie, please.'

Cade nodded, smiling his acceptance as he let her hand go with a faint reluctance before looking past her when Logan spoke harshly.

'Now that we've got the introductions out of the way, I suggest you tell me why you wanted to see me, Cade.'

There was no mistaking the authoritative note in Logan's voice, and Cade Rylance stiffened perceptibly.

For a moment the two men faced one another, tension humming in the air between them. Stephanie stared from one set face to the other, wondering what was going on, then suddenly Cade gave a faint shrug, a trace of wry amusement on his face. 'Just thought you'd like to know that Dream Dancer has dropped her foal. Looks like a winner to me. Could be that your money and my know-how has paid off.'

Some of the tension seemed to ease from Logan, although his voice still held an edge of steel. 'About time too! I'll be out to see them both in a few minutes.'

Cade accepted the dismissal, although there was still a trace of amusement about his smile as he glanced briefly at Stephanie before disappearing as quietly as he'd appeared. She let out her breath slowly, suddenly aware that she'd been holding it in check. What had been going on between Logan and his manager just now? She glanced at Logan, but he'd already turned away to open the huge walk-in wardrobe set into the wall opposite the bed. He took out a smart dark grey suit and laid it on the bed, then glanced up at where she stood uncertainly by the door.

'Was there something else?'

'I... No.' She shook her head, feeling the long silky hair suddenly slipping from the pins she'd fastened it with on top of her head. Quickly she pulled them out, then shook her hair free, feeling it swirling around her shoulders before she smoothed it behind her ears and looked back at Logan. Her heart seemed to stop dead, hard and heavy in her chest, as she saw the expression on his face. Then it was gone so fast that she knew she'd imagined it, a view confirmed by the ice that crackled in his harsh voice.

'Then I suggest that you get out of here...unless you're offering to help me change?' He dragged the shirt over his head, then tossed it onto the bed, smiling when he saw the expression of shock on her face. She didn't want to stare at him, didn't *want* to let him see how the sight of his broad, muscular chest with its thick covering of dark gold hair over deeply tanned skin affected her, but she seemed powerless to turn away.

'It could be a nice idea, honey.' His voice had dropped an octave, dark and infinitely dangerous now. 'Perhaps I'm being foolish to resist your charms after all. Mixing business with pleasure could be a whole new experience, a very pleasant one at that!'

It was the mockery that got through to her at last, the deliberate taunt. She drew herself upright, her face so pale that it seemed ethereal in the sharp, clear light pouring into the room. 'Go to hell, Logan Ford, and take your horrible ideas with you!'

She turned to leave, forcing herself to walk slowly and purposefully out of the door, but she wasn't proof against the sound of his mocking laughter. With a tiny stifled cry, she ran. She hated him! Hated, loathed and detested everything about him! The words raced through her head, but they weren't loud enough to block out the sound of his laugh. It seemed to echo right through her, mocking her attempts to relegate him to a position of just being an irritating nuisance in her life. He was more than that, much, much more, but there was no way that she was going to make the mistake of deciding exactly what!

CHAPTER FIVE

STEPHANIE was outside playing ball with Jessica when Logan appeared, dressed in the dark grey suit and a grey and white striped shirt. His dark red hair was smoothly brushed back from his forehead, his freshly shaved face deeply tanned. He looked rich and powerful and so very, very attractive that Stephanie dropped the ball that Jessica had thrown to her.

'Butter fingers!' Jessica whirled away to retrieve it from the grass, then stopped to admire a brightly coloured butterfly that was flitting in and out of a nearby tub of flowers. Stephanie glanced almost desperately towards the child, but before she could call out to her to come back and carry on with the game Logan had arrived at her side.

'I shall be away for the whole afternoon, possibly until the early evening. Do you think you'll be able to cope?' There was a faint concern as he glanced back at his daughter, and Stephanie hurried to reassure him.

'Of course. There's no need to worry. I'm well used to dealing with children, don't forget. I taught at a boarding-school before I went on that extended holiday; that meant me coming into far closer contact with the children than a teacher usually does.'

'I know that.' He must have seen the flicker of surprise that crossed her face, because he smiled thinly. 'My enquiries were extensive, Stephanie. I contacted the school and eventually tracked down your former headmistress to ask her about you. It was partly due to her recommendation that you're here.'

'But who gave you permission to do that? I didn't!'

He seemed unperturbed by her anger, his dark eyes cool as they studied her angry face. 'I didn't need your permission. I was hardly going to entrust my daughter to just anyone.'

It was so typical of him, of course: he would never ask permission from anyone, just set about getting what he wanted with scant regard for a person's feelings! 'I still think that you overstepped the mark, Mr Ford. It is usual to seek references *after* a job has been filled, not before.'

'There wasn't time to bother with the niceties. I needed to know if you would be suitable and set about finding out as fast as I could.' He slipped a hand into the pocket of his suit jacket, obviously putting an end to that line of conversation. 'Take this card. It's the number where I can be reached if you need to contact me. Feel free to call me at any time.'

Stephanie took the printed card, glancing curiously down at it, her brow puckering in surprise. 'Ford Construction? Is that what you do, construction work? But I thought this must be the line of business you were in.' She waved a hand round to indicate the rolling green fields where horses grazed under the hot sun.

He laughed softly, following her gaze. 'This is my hobby, Stephanie. A rather expensive hobby, admittedly, but perhaps it's going to start paying off if what Rylance said about that foal is true.'

'Hobby?' Startled, she stared back at him, then let her eyes drift once more to the backdrop of fields, the impressive stable block she could just see to the rear of the house. She knew nothing at all about horses, but she didn't need to to realise that this kind of a set-up must cost a fortune to maintain.

'Mmm. It was a reward, if you like to call it that, to myself for all the years of hard work.' There was pride in his harsh voice, a sense of achievement as he stared across the rolling meadows. 'I came from nothing, and everything I have now I've earned by sheer hard work.'

'In the construction world?' She kept her voice quiet, wanting to learn something more about this man, yet afraid that he would shy away from answering any questions as he usually seemed to do.

'Yes. It's been a long haul, a difficult one too, but I made it. Ford Construction is involved in a host of different projects throughout Florida, ranging from small retirement homes to hotels and shopping malls. Florida has always attracted a high percentage of retirees, drawn here by the climate. Latest figures estimate that some nine hundred plus arrive each day, and they all need housing, facilities, et cetera. Add to that figure the expanding tourist market, and you can see for yourself that construction work ranks as one of the major industries.' He glanced down at her, his eyes hooded now as they studied the interest on her face. 'I am a rich man, Stephanie, a very rich man. I can afford to indulge my dreams.'

And his dream had been to make money. Stephanie saw the answer in his face and for some reason it made her ache. He'd obviously achieved all he had set out to do, but at what cost? He was a man who had everything, yet had nothing apart from his daughter, and even that relationship seemed to be overshadowed by painful memories. Unconsciously her voice softened at the thought. 'Well, don't worry about Jessica. I shall take good care of her, Logan.'

He seemed to draw back behind the barrier he'd erected between himself and the world, or was it only with her that he was so guarded? 'That's what you're here to do. As I said, call me if you have problems; otherwise you should find everything you need in the house. I'm afraid your duties will include making meals for yourself and Jessica, as the housekeeper I had hired to cook and care for her let me down. But it shouldn't prove to be too great a problem. One of the farm-hands' wife cleans the house and stocks the refrigerator.' He pushed his cuff back to glance at the expensive gold watch that circled his broad wrist. 'I have to go now. Don't forget, any problems then——'

'Call you.' She smiled brittly, hiding the ache she felt at the way he had so ruthlessly slotted her back into her allotted role. 'Don't worry; I shall cope. I dare say I can always find Cade Rylance if I have a major problem and need immediate assistance in caring for an eight-year-old child!'

She'd meant to be sarcastic, to let him know that she resented his high-handed issuing of orders as though she were some half-wit incapable of dealing with even the most minor occurrence. It surprised her to see anger in his eyes out of all proportion to her comments.

He moved a step closer, towering over her. 'Keep out of Rylance's way, honey. Understand? He's hired to do a job, the same as you are. I'm not paying you both good money to spend your time making out!'

Of all the nerve! He was virtually accusing her of planning on starting up an affair with his manager on the strength of a few polite words of introduction!

Stephanie opened her mouth to let rip, then fell silent when he just turned and strode away without another word, letting her know that as far as he was concerned that was the end of it. He had issued his orders, and she was meant to follow them to the letter! Had he been born with such arrogance, or had he acquired it along with his wealth? She had no way of knowing, just the certainty that taking him down a peg or two would be an achievement she would relish!

The day flew past. After their ball game, Jessica begged to play in the pool, and Stephanie didn't have the heart to refuse her. There was something extremely appealing about the child that stemmed from the strange mixture of confidence and uncertainty she exhibited in almost equal measures. One minute she would be laughing and playing like any other eight-year-old, but the next the slightest word could upset her. By the time evening came, Stephanie was learning to monitor every word she said in case Jessica didn't realise that she was teasing her. Perhaps it was just a case that the child was as yet still unsure of her, but something told her that the problem ran deeper than that.

Around six o'clock she made them both a light meal from the vast selection of food she discovered in the huge double-doored refrigerator. The kitchen was a marvel of science, every labour-saving device she could wish for installed in the antique pine cupboards, yet none of them looked as though they had ever been used. When she switched on the grill to cook the lamb chops she'd found in the freezer, there was the unmistakable odour of newness issuing from the sleek fitment as the grill heated up.

Jessica ate every scrap of the meal, then sat back with a sigh. 'That was lovely, Stephie. Almost as good as Teresa's meals.'

'And who's Teresa? One of your friends' mothers?' Stephanie asked the question distractedly as she piled the dishes on to the draining-board and peered into the gleaming interior of the dishwasher, wondering if it was worth trying to fathom out how to operate it.

'No, silly!' Jessica laughed in delight, scrambling from the chair to open the fridge and take out a carton of ice-cream. 'She's Grandma's cook, of course. Can I have some of this, please?'

'I... yes, of course.' Startled by the piece of information, Stephanie left the dishwasher and handed the child a bowl, watching while she scooped ice-cream from the tub.

'Do you want some, Stephie? It's good.' Jessica licked the spoon to emphasise the point, then set it down when Stephanie shook her head. Stephanie waited until the child had sat down at the table again, then couldn't help herself from probing deeper.

'Is Grandma your daddy's mother?'

'No. Daddy's parents are both dead. I never saw them.'

'But you see your grandma, do you?'

'I used to. I used to stay at Grandma's house a lot, and Teresa would take me to the beach to play, but since... since Mummy died I haven't been there.' She set the spoon down with a clatter, her small face suddenly sad. 'I miss them both, Stephanie. Do you think you could ask Daddy if I can go visit them some time?'

She'd do more than that! What on earth was Logan thinking of by cutting the child off from all contact with her maternal grandparents? She forced a smile, anxious to wipe the unhappiness from Jessica's face. 'I certainly shall, but only if you promise not to brood about it. OK?'

The child studied her in silence, then picked up the spoon and attacked the ice-cream with gusto. 'OK. I'm glad you're here, Stephanie. Really glad. I hope Daddy lets you stay forever!'

Stephanie turned away to hide her sudden tears at the touching assertion, wondering what Logan would make of that idea. He might be willing to tolerate her for a few weeks, but for longer than that...? She ran water into the sink and washed the dishes, telling herself not to be so sentimental and foolish. She was here to do a job, that was all, and, by doing that, get herself out of a fix. She was just being silly to wish suddenly that she could in some way become a permanent part of Jessica's life. That it would naturally entail her becoming part of Logan's life as well was something she didn't stop to dwell on.

She was half asleep when the sound of heavy footsteps on the hall floor roused her. Jumping up from the settee, she started towards the door, wondering why she'd not heard the sound of a car. Jessica had been increasingly restless as the time had passed and still Logan hadn't come back, and it had taken all Stephanie's ingenuity and patience to keep her occupied. Finally, at a little before nine, when the child's eyelids were drooping, she'd cajoled her into going up to bed, adding the reassurance that Logan would be there in the morning when she woke up. Now there was a light of battle in her blue eyes as she went to waylay him at the door and let him know what she thought of his tardiness.

She stepped out into the hall then stopped abruptly, one hand flying to her mouth to stem the cry when she saw the man coming towards her. In the faint light spilling from the sitting-room she failed to recognise him at first, just knew at once that it wasn't Logan.

'Miss Jacobs... it's me, Cade Rylance. I didn't mean to give you a scare, ma'am.'

She gave a little laugh, relief making her go weak as she recognised the dark-haired man. 'It's all right. I'd been dozing off and just didn't realise it was you. If you want Mr Ford, then I'm afraid he isn't back yet.'

Cade moved towards her, a hint of apology still glowing in his green eyes. 'I know that. There was no sign of his car, so I thought I'd just check you were all right before I turned in for the night. It can be kind of daunting being left all alone in a strange place.'

His consideration warmed her, being such a direct contrast to the way Logan treated her, and she smiled at him with genuine appreciation. 'Thank you. That was very kind. Would you like some coffee while you're here? I could do with a cup.'

'If you're sure it's no trouble.'

'Of course not. I'd be glad of the company, to tell the truth.'

He stepped aside so that she could precede him along the passage to the kitchen, then stood uncertainly in the doorway. Stephanie filled the coffee-maker, then turned to grin at him. 'Well, come on in, then. I don't bite!'

He laughed softly, a melodic sound that was strangely soothing. 'I'm sure you don't. I was just wondering whether it was wise or not. Logan didn't seem to take to the idea of my speaking to you earlier on today.'

There was a polite question in the man's deep, soft voice, but it still brought the colour into Stephanie's face. She turned away to take two cups from the cupboard, keeping her face averted from the searching green gaze. 'I'm sure you imagined that, Mr Rylance. I explained to you what my position is here. I'm sure that Logan...Mr Ford's main concern is that I do my job!'

'I'm sure it is.' There was faint amusement in Cade's tone, and Stephanie felt an answering smile creeping up on her. She set the cups down on the table and then looked at him with a wry grimace.

'You seem to know Logan extremely well.'

He spooned sugar into his cup, then took a sip of the hot liquid before answering. 'Better than most, I expect. Logan and I go a long way back. That's the reason why I'm always wary of that red-haired devil's temper!'

Stephanie laughed out loud, turning back to the fridge to fill a jug with milk before sitting down opposite him at the table and pouring some into her coffee. 'An apt description! Although I doubt that you're afraid of him, Mr Rylance.'

'Make that Cade; and no, I'm not. I've just learned to respect him and give him the space he needs.' He shrugged lightly, a hint of his previous curiosity showing briefly on his face. 'How come he hired you to take care of Jess? I thought he was going to Orlando to have a holiday, not start hiring himself staff.'

'I expect he was. I just happened along his path and he saw an opportunity to solve a problem.' As briefly as she could she explained the circumstances of her meeting with Logan, then paused, wondering if she was being pushy by asking a few questions of her own.

'I know so little about what happened—to Jessica's mother, that is. Yet I have a feeling that so much hinges on her. What was she like?'

For a moment she thought he wasn't going to answer her, then he spoke in a deliberately controlled voice. 'On the outside she was probably the most beautiful woman I've ever seen, but on the inside she was as cold and ugly as sin.'

Stephanie gasped. 'You can't really mean that.'

'I can and I do. Amanda could turn a man's head all right, make him want her, then once he had her he'd soon regret it.'

'Did...did Logan feel that way?' She knew she shouldn't be questioning the man like this, asking about things she had no real right to know, but some deep desire to learn more about Logan drove her on.

However, it seemed that Cade was already regretting what he'd said. He drained the hot coffee, then set the cup back down and stood up. 'I guess that's the sort of question that only Logan himself can answer, and I very much doubt that he'd appreciate my doing it for him.'

Feeling rebuked, Stephanie stood up too, faint colour tinging her cheeks. 'I'm sorry. I should never have put you in such an awkward position by asking it in the first place.'

'It's only natural to be interested in your...employer.' There was a faint but marked hesitation in the statement but before Stephanie could even start to assure him that that was all Logan was to her the front door opened and footsteps echoed along the hallway. She stepped nervously away from the table, the colour ebbing from her face when Logan stopped in the doorway to the room. In a fast-assessing sweep his eyes took in the two coffee-cups, then lifted to Stephanie with an undisguised contempt.

'This looks cosy. You and Cade been getting better acquainted, then?' It was the way he said that, his harsh voice echoing with meaning. Stephanie stiffened at once, glaring back at him, but it was Cade Rylance who spoke first.

'I stopped by to check everything was all right when I saw your car wasn't back. Stephanie kindly made me a cup of coffee.'

The air seemed to be charged with tension as the two men stared at each other, but in the end it was Cade who turned away first. He gave Stephanie a brief smile, then nodded at Logan. 'I shall see you tomorrow, I expect. I'll be going over to that sale to see if I can pick up a couple of new brood mares; you need to tell me what figures I'm working around.'

Logan said nothing, barely acknowledging the other man had even spoken, his whole attention centred on Stephanie. She met his gaze proudly, refusing to be browbeaten into feeling guilty at what he'd walked in on. She'd done nothing wrong in inviting the farm manager in for coffee!

After Cade left with a murmured goodnight, she picked up the cups from the table and started to carry them to the sink, then stopped abruptly when Logan's hand closed around her arm.

'I told you what I expected from you. Didn't I make myself clear enough? If not, then maybe I'd better repeat it: I don't want you chasing after my manager!'

She glared at him, her blue eyes filled with fire, her heart aching. 'I wasn't chasing anyone! Cade dropped by to see if I needed anything, that's all.'

He dropped her arm and stepped back, staring at her with icy mockery. 'Now what on earth could you possibly need? You have everything here, honey. Apart from a little male company, that is. Maybe that's what you were so desperate for. Are you the sort of woman who can't live without that?'

She set the cups down, afraid that she would drop them because she was shaking so much. How dared he? 'I can live perfectly happily without male company, thank you very much. Especially without yours! It's no damned wonder your wife left you, Logan Ford. It must be difficult to live with a man who's ice through to the core!'

There was a moment, just one, when her words seemed to hang in the air between them. Stephanie could scarcely believe what she'd just said, but there was no way to take it back. She held her breath as she waited to feel the full force of the wrath she could see building inside him, knowing that she deserved it. How could she have said that to him? The moment stretched until it could stretch no further, the tension building to volcanic proportions. Then as Logan took one slow step towards her a scream cut through the air, a scream of such terror that both of them jumped.

'Jessica!' The single word was gritted out between clenched teeth, Logan's face betraying a mixture of anger and fear as he turned and ran along the hall towards the stairs. Stephanie grabbed hold of the chair-back, clinging to it as weakness claimed her. It took every ounce of courage she possessed to let go of the solid wood and follow him, but somehow she managed it. It wasn't over, of course. Logan would never let her get away with what she'd said, but for now there was Jessica to attend to.

It took over an hour to soothe the child and settle her back to sleep. Stephanie watched helplessly while Logan held his daughter, his voice filled with tenderness as he murmured to her. He loved the child so much, that was obvious, and startling in a way when one considered what a cold man he appeared to be on the surface. It made her wonder once again if that coldness was just a way to hide his true emotions. What would it be like to get past that barrier and touch the flame she sensed hidden inside him? Just the thought scared her.

Strangely unsettled, she muttered an excuse to leave, offering to fetch Jessica a drink rather than stay there in the room any longer while her mind explored avenues it had no right to go along. But as soon as Jessica heard what she said she re-doubled her sobs. Launching herself from Logan's arms, she clung to Stephanie, her small body heaving.

Stephanie sat on the edge of the bed, smoothing the tumbled hair back from her hot, damp cheeks, her whole attention focused on quietening Jessica's fears now, so that she started nervously when Logan suddenly spoke.

'I think she'll sleep now. See if she will lie down for you.' There was a throbbing ache in the harsh tones which told her clearly how he hated to see his daughter like this. Stephanie glanced at him over Jessica's head, unconsciously holding the child just a shade closer.

'She will be all right, Logan.'

'Will she? I wish to God I had your confidence!'

The child stirred restlessly at the anger in his voice, her sleepy eyelids drifting open. 'Daddy?'

'I'm here, Jess. I'll be here all night long, honey.'

'Promise?'

He ruffled her red curls, his touch so tender that Stephanie had to turn away as tears misted her eyes at the poignancy of watching this strong, indomitable man with the vulnerable child.

'Of course I promise, but only if you promise to go back to sleep. You have a busy day tomorrow. I want you to choose a name for Dream Dancer's foal.'

Jessica smiled, the last of her fear easing from her face as she let Stephanie tuck her up, but when Stephanie turned to leave she clung to her hand. 'You haven't kissed me goodnight, Stephie.'

Stephanie smiled, deeply touched by the request. 'How could I have forgotten that? Silly me.' She bent and kissed the little girl's cheek, then stood up.

'Now Daddy. You have to kiss him goodnight too.'

It was such an innocent request, yet it started up a storm inside her. Stephanie looked at Logan, feeling her heart racing at the thought. He raised a mocking brow, his eyes hooded as he watched her in a silence which seemed to resound with so many unspoken words and feelings that she felt giddy. She swallowed hard, then glanced back at Jessica, almost groaning when she saw the tension creeping into her face again.

'We don't want to keep Jess awake all night, do we?'

He must have known how she was feeling, known and been enjoying the dilemma it put her in! Stephanie glared at him as she walked the few steps it took to reach him and press her lips against the hardness of his cheek. She stepped away at once, barely stopping to wish Jessica another goodnight before she hurried from the room and ran down the stairs. She stopped at the bottom to press a fingertip to her tingling mouth, feeling again the abrasive warmth of Logan's skin.

'I could do with a drink after that, and I expect you could too.' He came down the stairs, and she hurriedly dropped her hand as she moved aside so that he could pass her.

'I... No. Thank you. I don't want anything. I think I would prefer to go up to bed if you don't mind.'

'But I do mind.' He stopped beside her, his eyes cutting deep into hers. 'I want an explanation of what's been going on here, and I want it now!' He opened the door to what was obviously his study, waiting for her to precede him before following her and closing it again with a restrained violence.

Walking over to a table holding an assortment of drinks, he poured whiskey into a glass and took a deep swallow before setting the glass aside. 'Now let's hear it. Exactly what has been going on here to get Jessica in such a state?'

He was actually blaming *her* for the child's nightmares! Stephanie stood up and stared coldly back at him across the width of the room. 'I imagine that Jessica was upset because you were so late. She was fine all afternoon long, but when you failed to appear at the given time then she started getting increasingly restless.'

'Then why the hell didn't you phone me? Dammit, woman, why do you think I went to such pains to impress upon you that you should phone me if there was a problem? Was it too much to expect you to handle a simple request like that?'

His anger was building, daunting in its speed and ferocity, but Stephanie stood her ground. 'I didn't call you because I didn't see that it *was* a problem! Naturally Jessica would be a bit concerned because you were late, but I never imagined that it would cause that much of an upset!'

'You never imagined? And that's your excuse for your incompetence, is it?' He picked up the glass, then drained the whiskey, glaring at her as he set it back down on the tray. 'Are you quite sure that is the only reason you failed to call me?'

'Of course! What other reason would I have had?'

'Cade Rylance for one.' He smiled slowly, his dark eyes glittering with contempt as he moved across the room towards her. 'Why call me and urge me to come back home when you had other plans, eh? Getting to know my manager must have been a far more attractive proposition than caring for that child!'

Even days later she didn't know why she did it, couldn't explain what prompted her to choose a course of action that common sense should have warned her against. All she knew was that one minute Logan was standing there glaring down at her, and the next her hand was flying up to slap his face with all the force she could muster.

'Why, you little...' The rest of what he'd been about to say was cut off as he caught her by the shoulders and hauled her against him, his hands biting deep into her flesh as he held her and took her mouth in a kiss of such ferocity that she whimpered under the bruising force of it. Stephanie tried desperately to turn her head to avoid his mouth, but he wouldn't let her as he raised his hand and twined his fingers into her hair to hold her in place. Then suddenly he pushed her away from him and stepped back, running the back of his hand across his mouth as though to erase the taste of her.

Stephanie stumbled back, catching hold of the desk to steady herself as her legs threatened to give way. She was shaking so much that she could hardly stand, her whole body trembling with a fine, tight tension that threatened to snap at any moment. She ran a hand over her burning, bruised lips, her eyes haunted as they lifted to his set face. 'You...you had no right to do that...no right!'

He stared back at her, his eyes lingering just for a second on the swollen redness of her mouth before meeting hers without the faintest trace of apology. 'And you had no right to slap me, so that makes us even.'

There was a bitter, twisted logic in his words, but it didn't help ease the pain she felt at the way he had treated her with such contempt. Tears swam in her eyes, and she turned abruptly away so that he couldn't see them, staring down at the smooth, polished wood of the huge desk. The silence seemed to stretch between them, and suddenly she couldn't stand it any longer.

'You were wrong, Logan, about tonight. I didn't plan on inviting Cade in for coffee, nor did I put off calling you because he arrived. I...I just never realised that Jessica was so upset.' She turned to look at him then, willing him to understand, and saw something flicker in those shuttered eyes before he walked away to refill his glass.

'I see.'

'Do you?' She laughed suddenly, then bit her lip, using the instant pain to quell the momentary hysteria. 'Then you understand more than I do. That's the real problem, isn't it? You've told me so little about Jessica and...and her mother and what happened. It's unfair to expect me to cope with any problems that arise when I'm so much in the dark.'

He swirled the whiskey round the glass, studying the shimmering patterns of gold it made, then suddenly set the glass down on the tray with a thump that reverberated around the room and made her jump. 'So you believe that I should have told you more, do you?'

Stephanie nodded, wondering why she should suddenly feel afraid at what she might hear. She needed to know if she was to help Jessica through the next few weeks. But what would Logan tell her?

'I won't bore you with all the detail, just the facts that have a bearing on what has happened to Jessica recently.' His voice was flat, quite emotionless, yet Stephanie understood with a sudden perception that that was the only way he could handle whatever had happened. Emotion was something that he shied away from at all costs.

She said nothing, waiting for him to continue, and after a brief second he carried on. 'Amanda died three months ago. She was on one of her frequent holidays at the time. She had little to fill her days with apart from finding new ways to enjoy herself, and she excelled at that.' He paused to sip the whiskey, his hands steady as he cradled the glass and looked back at something that was obviously a source of pain to him. Stephanie was both shocked and amazed at the control he showed, that iron will-power. What had shaped Logan into the man he was today? What hardships and hurts had taught him to hide his feelings behind that icy exterior? She ached to know, then was glad she didn't, realising that in some strange way it would have hurt *her* to discover what he'd been through.

'So where was Amanda when she died? How did she die?' Her voice was quiet, in keeping with the mood, and he barely glanced at her as he answered.

'She was killed in an automobile accident, driving while under the influence of too much alcohol. As for where it happened, that doesn't matter. It could have been anywhere at all, anywhere that took her fancy, and with anyone.' He smiled when he saw her shock. 'Did I fail to mention that? Not that it makes much difference, but Amanda had one of her many admirers in tow.'

'And Jessica... was she involved in the crash? Is that what causes her nightmares?'

'No. Jessica had been left behind at the lodge Amanda had hired, while she and her boyfriend went out for the night. But they didn't come back, you see. They had that accident and that was it. No one realised there was a child left behind, waiting, watching, wondering when her mother was going to come back for her.' Suddenly he hurled the glass across the room, watching dispassionately as it shattered against the wall in a rainbow explosion of glass. 'My daughter was left on her own for almost twenty-four hours until the maid came by to clean the lodge and found her!'

'Oh, but that's dreadful! No wonder she has nightmares and she was so worried when you didn't return home on time.'

'Yes, no wonder. Now perhaps you will understand why it is so important to call me. I didn't intend to be so late, but there were several problems that urgently required my attention. When you didn't call I assumed that everything was all right here. Obviously I was mistaken.'

He was still apportioning her the major part of the blame, but it was so unfair. 'If I had known all the facts, then naturally I would have phoned. You should have explained all this to me sooner!' There was a glint of challenge in her blue eyes, and for a moment he stiffened, then slowly walked across the room to sink down on to the huge brown leather sofa and stretch his long legs in front of him with a sigh.

'Perhaps I should. I'm prepared to give you the benefit of the doubt this time, Stephanie.'

That was big of him! 'Thank you so much, Mr Ford. That's really kind of you. Are you sure there isn't anything else I need to know so that I won't make any future errors?'

The sweetly coated sarcasm got through to him immediately. He stared back at her, his handsome face set, a nerve ticking along his lean jaw. 'Don't push me too far, honey. You might not like the reaction you get.'

A *frisson* ran down her spine, a tiny warning she dismissed with a toss of her head. 'Is that so? Well, if it's anything like the reaction I got before, then I'm sure I wouldn't!'

He laughed softly, menacingly, as he came to his feet and moved towards her, standing so close that she could feel the warmth of his breath against her cheek. Reaching out, he trailed a hard finger down her nose, then let it stop on the red swell of her lips, still tender from the bruising kiss. 'Next time the punishment would be more subtle, Stephanie. It isn't always necessary to use force to get a point across.'

Her breath seemed to stop, her chest aching with the pressure as she stared up into those hypnotically dark eyes and read the message in them. Then with a shuddering little moan she pushed past him and hurried towards the door.

'Oh, just one thing you should know, Stephanie. Amanda didn't leave me, nor did she divorce me because of my unreasonable behaviour.'

His voice and what he said stopped her in her tracks and she looked back, watching as he sat back down on the sofa, his head resting against the soft leather. He seemed to be waiting for her to speak, but for the life of her Stephanie couldn't find the words to ask the question she was aching to hear the answer to. He must have read her mind, because he smiled suddenly in that mocking way she was learning to hate.

'I'm sure you are just being polite by not asking me to explain, exhibiting that famous British reserve. So let me tell you, to spare your finer feelings. Amanda and I were never married. We were together for some time, but I never made the mistake of taking her for my wife.' The mockery faded, his face like stone. 'There isn't a woman born who could make me want to give that kind of commitment.'

Stephanie turned and walked out of the room, holding herself rigid against a pain that seemed to have no basis in logic. It should make no difference to her what Logan had just admitted. Why should she care that he intended to spend his life alone without any kind of commitment? *Why*? It was that one question that was destined to haunt her that night and for many nights to come; the one question she would never dare to search for an answer to.

CHAPTER SIX

IT WAS a little after six in the morning when Stephanie walked into the kitchen. She'd barely slept, her mind too busy with everything that Logan had told her. Walking over to the sink, she filled the coffee-maker and started a pot of coffee, needing the stimulus it might give her to clear her head of the lingering memories.

She'd just poured a first cup and set it down on the table when the sound of footsteps echoing along the hall made her swing round, her heart thumping painfully fast when Logan came into the room. He paused in the doorway, obviously surprised to find her there, then calmly walked over and filled himself a cup of the fragrant brew. Leaning a hip against the worktop, he studied her in silence while he took a cautious sip of the burning liquid.

Stephanie sat down abruptly at the table, lowering her eyes to her cup as she stirred the coffee round and round, but after several minutes' silence found she couldn't help but glance back at him. In a fast sweep her eyes skimmed his leanly powerful body, taking stock of the washed-smooth denim jeans that clung lovingly to his long legs, the pale blue chambray shirt that he'd left partly unbuttoned. He was as devastatingly attractive in the casual clothes as he had been the day before in the expensive formal suit, and she hated the way her body reacted to the sight of him with a hot surge of awareness.

'Are you always such an early riser?' His voice was husky with the remnants of sleep, grating disturbingly along nerves already stretched almost to breaking-point. Stephanie took a heartening sip of the strong coffee, then gave a tiny shrug. 'I couldn't sleep. Probably being in a strange place and a strange bed, I expect.'

It was such a blatant lie, and she knew at once that he realised that. He smiled faintly, cradling the cup in his hand as he raised it to his mouth again, then set it down while he re-filled it. 'I would have imagined that you'd be well used to sleeping in strange beds by now, Stephanie.'

She stiffened at once, instantly imagining the worst in what he said, then blushed when he laughed and added quietly, 'I meant with you travelling around Europe. Nothing else, honey.'

It was the first time that he'd employed that particular note of teasing banter with her, and she wasn't proof against the fiery heat that ran along her veins. Abruptly she stood up and walked across the room to re-fill her own cup, using the few minutes it took to get her wayward emotions in hand again. 'I'm sure you did. However, strange though it may sound, I still have difficulty in adapting to fresh places. Probably stems from the fact that I'm a home body at heart.'

'Yet you still decided to spend...how many months travelling around?' There was a note almost of censure in his voice now that startled her slightly because she couldn't understand the reason for it.

'Just because I made up my mind to see something of the world doesn't mean that I would want to keep on wandering all the time. It was an experience, one I wouldn't have missed for anything, and I'm glad that I plucked up enough courage to go through with it. And that I managed to persuade Laura and Rachel to come along. I think we all learned a lot from the past six months, but that doesn't mean that I'm not looking forward to going home again.'

'I wonder if you'll find it that easy to do.' He shook his head, the light from the window setting fire to the red-gold of his hair. 'I doubt it. Settling back into the boredom of everyday life will be twice as hard now that you've had that taste of freedom.'

She wasn't sure she liked the way he said that, the faint note of condemnation. As far as she was concerned, the decision to see something of the world had been one of the best she'd ever made. Now she could settle back down to earning a living and building a life for herself without always wondering what she'd missed. But obviously Logan didn't see it that way. However, before she could say anything else he suddenly tipped the rest of the coffee down the sink and rinsed his cup, setting it to drain on the rack. There was a leashed tension about his movements, far removed from that brief moment of camaraderie they'd shared before they'd moved on to the subject of her travels. It made her curious to find out the reason for it.

'Is there something wrong, Logan? Have I said something to annoy you?' She laughed shakily. 'I can't imagine what, although it doesn't seem to take much where I'm concerned!'

He stared back at her, arrogance etched all over his hard-boned face. 'I'm not annoyed, Stephanie, and, as for your seeming to have some sort of strange ability to annoy me, I'm glad to say that you're mistaken. You're here to do a job, and personal feelings don't enter into it at all.'

'Don't they?' She stiffened, her eyes burning back at him. 'I'd say that is an out-and-out lie, and you know it!'

'And *I* would say that you are starting to imagine things...probably because you're tired and overwrought after last night's little episode with Jessica. What you need, Stephanie, is some fresh air to set you back on course. Come along.'

He pulled her up from the chair, taking the cup from her hand and setting it down on the table as he started to lead her towards the back door.

'Just a minute! Where are we going?' She hung back, strangely reluctant to let him organise her like this without making even a token protest. To give an inch to Logan Ford was to give ten miles!

'Out to the stables to see Dancer and her foal.' He smiled suddenly, so close to her now that she received the full force of it somewhere in her solar plexus, making her breath catch and the rest of her protests die a sudden death. 'There's nothing like the miracle of new life to put everything into perspective, I find.'

'I... But what about Jessica?' It was just a token attempt at protest now, just a last desperate way to cling hold of common sense. If she was to survive these coming weeks unscathed then she had to remember why she was here and try to avoid spending too much time in Logan's company. He was far too disturbing for her peace of mind.

'She won't wake up for a couple of hours yet. Those damned nightmares usually take their toll all right. But we won't be that long anyway.'

He opened the door and stepped out into the warmth of the early morning air, and slowly Stephanie followed him, forcing a slight smile to her stiff lips when he glanced round at her. He led her away from the house towards the stable block, unlocking the heavily padlocked gate to let himself into the yard. A man appeared from a doorway, but he merely waved when he recognised Logan and went back inside. Logan must have seen the curiosity on Stephanie's face, because he smiled a trifle grimly. 'The horses we keep here are all thoroughbreds, very expensive animals. We have to be careful about security at all times, so I have several men employed solely for that purpose.'

'I see.' She shivered suddenly. 'How horrible to think that you need to do that.'

He shrugged dismissively. 'I imagine that it isn't unknown for something similar to happen even in England. Racehorses and the breeding of them is big business and can attract the wrong kind of attention.'

'But you said you did this just as a hobby.' She followed him towards the far row of stables, standing back as he unbolted the doors to a loose box.

'It is, but that doesn't mean to say I wouldn't enjoy making a profit from it. If a job is worth doing, then it's worth doing to the best of one's ability. Now look.' He guided her into the stable, closing the door quietly behind them as a precaution, but the huge grey mare didn't seem at all perturbed by their sudden intrusion. She whickered softly through her nostrils, shoving her head against Logan's shoulder before snuffling delicately at his jeans pockets as she searched for treats. He laughed gently and rubbed her forehead.

'Nothing for you at the moment, Dancer, you clever girl. Better luck next time, eh?'

Losing interest, the mare moved away, stepping carefully through the thick bedding of straw, and that was when Stephanie caught sight of the foal. Even as she watched, it suddenly struggled up on its spindly little legs and stood swaying perilously for a second, staring at them from huge dark eyes before turning to its mother and starting to feed.

'Oh, it's so beautiful, Logan.' Stephanie's voice was low so as not to disturb the pair, but she couldn't hide the pleasure she felt at the scene they made. She glanced up at him, her face alight, her eyes sparkling, and felt the blood roar into her head as she met his dark gaze in a look of such intensity that the whole world seemed to stop. Sensation arced between them in a surge of rawly primitive force, joining them for one brief moment out of eternity so that she felt that she was part of him and that he was part of her.

'Logan...' His name was half-question, half-plea as she whispered it softly in the silence. She repeated it, wanting to taste and feel the sound of it on her lips. 'Logan.' She took a hesitant step towards him, then stopped abruptly when he spoke.

'We'd better go. I don't want Dancer disturbed too much at present, not if what Rylance said is true.' His eyes shifted from her face, centring on the mare and foal with such cold calculation in their depths that Stephanie almost cried out in protest. 'That animal represents a lot of money.'

It was such a deliberate rejection of what had passed between them, made so coldly, so clinically, that she felt almost violated by it. Without a word she followed him out of the stable and carried on walking back to the house, uncaring that he made no attempt to follow her after he locked the door. She could search her heart forever and a day for an explanation of what had happened just now, that fierce, overwhelming bonding of one soul to another, but she would never find it. What she did know was that Logan had rejected what had happened with a deliberation that left no room for hope or dreams.

He had no interest in her; he'd stated it when he'd offered her this job and obviously he didn't intend to change his mind. She'd be a fool to let herself dream the situation would ever alter.

Jessica appeared little the worse for her disturbed night when she arrived downstairs an hour or so later. Stephanie had the feeling that the child remembered little of the night-time fears that had woken her, and she was glad. No child should have to bear that sort of a burden at such a tender age. It made her determined to do all she could to help Jessica over the next few weeks. It might not be a very long time, but surely she could provide the little girl with the stability that would go a long way to erasing her fears?

Pouring cereal into a bowl for the child, Stephanie put it on the table and smiled at her. 'I wasn't too certain what you ate for breakfast, but if you prefer to have something cooked then tomorrow I can make it for you.'

Jessica poured milk on to the cereal, then put the jug down just a second before it overflowed on to the table. 'We don't have a cooked breakfast because Daddy can't cook.'

Faintly surprised to have discovered something that Logan wasn't accomplished at, Stephanie smiled. 'I see.

So what happens about other meals? You can't eat cereal all the time, so does the lady who cleans the house make your meals?'

'Mary? Sometimes, but usually we go out to eat or put something in the microwave to heat up. Dad's good at that.'

Well, that explained the show-room newness of all the expensive equipment. Stephanie glanced round the huge kitchen, amusement lingering in her eyes as she turned back to Jessica. 'Well, if your father can't find a new housekeeper before I leave, then I had better offer to give him a few cookery lessons, don't you think?'

Jessica grinned. 'I can't imagine Daddy spending hours making a meal like Teresa does! He's always so busy with his business.'

'Mmm, well, I wasn't planning on anything elaborate. Just a few simple dishes that don't come out of a packet.'

'That sounds—— Morning, Dad.' Jessica scrambled from the table and ran to Logan as he suddenly appeared in the doorway. Catching hold of his hand, she swung backwards and forwards, laughing when he pretended to let her fall. 'Stephanie has said that she'll give you a few lessons.'

'She did? Doing what?' He looked across the room, the warmth still lingering in his dark eyes, and Stephanie hurriedly looked down at the cloth she was holding, folding it into perfect, precise creases. She couldn't forget what had happened before in the stable, and it made her suddenly self-conscious. What was it about Logan that put her on edge this way? She'd never had any hangups about dealing with the opposite sex before, but whenever they were together she was alarmingly aware of him as a man first, not just as another human being.

'What sort of lessons were you offering, teacher?' His voice seemed to be even deeper as he prompted her to answer, and she swallowed quickly to ease the knot in her throat.

'Just a few cookery lessons.' She looked up at him, then looked away just as quickly, her heart tapping furiously inside her chest. 'Jessica told me that you don't cook, so I thought it might help to show you a few simple meals.'

He shrugged lightly, loosening his hand from the child's grip as he moved further into the room. He hadn't changed out of the casual clothes, and as he stood next to her he seemed big and powerful and almost rawly masculine. 'I doubt if I need to learn. I've got by this long without cordon-bleu cookery. At any rate, I shall be interviewing for the housekeeping job within the next week, so there won't be a problem once I have someone hired. My secretary has already drawn up a list of suitable candidates.'

'I see.' Stephanie turned to rinse the cloth under the tap, her heart sinking at news that really wasn't any surprise. Being here was just a temporary measure to tide Logan over; it wasn't as if she would really want such a job full-time after all. She was a trained and experienced teacher, and now that she'd got that brief wanderlust out of her system she was looking forward to picking up where she'd left off. So why did she feel suddenly bitterly resentful of the woman who would eventually step into her shoes here in this house? It didn't make any sense, but there again she had the feeling that sense had gone winging out of the window the minute she'd met Logan Ford!

'I want you to concentrate all your attention on Jessica while you're here, Stephanie.' Logan's voice had dropped so that it wouldn't carry to the child, who was eating at the table, a chill in the harsh tones that brought Stephanie's head up.

'That's what I intend to do.'

'Good. I don't want you to start getting overly domesticated, worrying about cooking superb meals to impress me. Our contract is for a few short weeks, purely and simply as a convenience for me and to get you out of a difficult situation. Don't make the mistake of imagining it could become something more permanent, honey. I wouldn't like to see you disappointed.'

The sheer nerve of the man! He must have an ego as big as a mountain if he believed that! Pushing the fact that she had been pondering on that very idea to the back of her mind, Stephanie stared furiously at him. 'My God, but you do have an inflated opinion of your worth, don't you, Logan? I know it must be difficult for you to believe this, but not every woman you meet wants to throw herself at your feet before climbing into your bed!'

His eyes narrowed dangerously, glittering as they pinned her with a glance that scorched. 'Ego has little to do with it, lady!' He moved closer, his hand clamping over hers as she instinctively started to step back. Against the wetness of her skin, his fingers were cool and dry, iron-hard as he held her. 'I know how the female mind works. I've had a fair amount of experience of it, if you'd like the truth. Being here in my house could start giving a woman ideas along entirely the wrong lines. You're here to look after Jessica, not me.'

'Don't flatter yourself! I'd as soon stand by and watch you starve as whiz up some culinary marvel to tempt your palate!'

'Oh, I won't starve. There are any number of ladies both eager and willing to take care of me if I wish, without there being any strings attached to the offers.' His voice was a rough growl, his meaning blatantly apparent, and Stephanie cursed the ready colour that filled her face. She dragged her hand away from his and turned on the tap full blast, shoving the cloth under it. Scalding hot water ran over the back of her hand, and she gasped in pain as she snatched it away to safety, but the damage had already been done.

'Of all the damn fool things to do...' Logan cursed roughly, grasping her wrist as he turned on the cold tap then plunged her reddened hand into the icy water.

'Owww! That hurts even worse. Stop it.' She tried to twist her hand free, but his fingers tightened, encircling the delicate bones of her wrist as he held her hand under the water and glared into her tear-misted eyes.

'It will hurt a whole lot more if we don't cool it down. Hold still, woman. Do you want to end up with a blistered hand just because you're too damned stubborn to accept a little help when it's offered? The last thing I need is the inconvenience of ferrying you back and forth to hospital!'

And there she had it, in a nutshell, the *real* reason why he was concerned! He was protecting his investment, of course. Indignation dried the tears at once, and she stood rigidly as the water poured across the sore flesh, soothing the heat from it. 'I would hate to become a nuisance, Mr Ford, but don't worry. If it does turn into a case of my having to go to hospital, then rest assured that I shall take the bus rather than trouble you!'

He laughed suddenly, his fingers loosening their grip so that they seemed almost to caress her wrist rather than force it to stay in place. 'I thought that would stop the tears. Now keep your hand under that water for another couple of minutes, then it should have helped stop any blistering.'

He let her go and turned to speak to Jessica, who had been watching the scene with huge eyes. 'Do you think you could go and find me some of that spray to take the sting out of burns, Jess? It's in my bathroom cabinet, I think.'

Jessica jumped up, obviously pleased to be asked to help. She hurried from the kitchen, the sound of her racing footsteps echoing along the hall. Logan opened a drawer in one of the cabinets and took out a spotless white tea-towel, then carried it back to the sink. He turned off the tap, then took Stephanie's hand, gently patting it dry with the towel before studying it with a faint frown. 'It doesn't look too bad to me, but how does it feel?' He ran the ball of his thumb softly across the flesh, the touch so light that it was more an impression of sensation rather than anything else. Stephanie shivered in sudden response, avoiding his searching gaze as he looked up at her. 'Sorry, did that hurt?'

'No...not really. It...it's just a bit tender now, that's all, but I'm sure I'll live.' She tried to make a joke out of the situation, but had the sinking feeling it wasn't wholly successful. It was disturbing to have him hold her, touch her like this, and it was hard to hide that from him. When his thumb made another gentle sortie over her skin she held her breath, willing him not to hear the thunderous pounding of her heart, which sounded deafening to her sensitive ears.

'I'm sure you will, despite the fact that it's a touch redder than I'd like to see it after that soaking. I expect that owes more to the fact that you have such fine skin, Stephanie.'

Could he feel what was happening to her? Feel the blood pulsing through her veins, feel the heat that was starting to curl through her whole body? Deliberately she eased her hand away from his and stared down at it as though she found the sight fascinating, but it was hard to hide the tight note of tension in her voice when she spoke. 'It's a curse I've learned to live with. This sort of pale, fine skin runs in the family; I've often wished that I was born with something different, the sort of complexion that tans and withstands the sun.'

'I think you should consider yourself extremely fortunate. Most women would give a fortune to have skin like yours, the kind that looks marvellous without the help of cosmetics.'

The compliment cut a hole through her attempts at reserve, startling her by its sincerity. Curiously she glanced up at him, studying the rare softening of his face, then hurriedly tried to find something to say when she suddenly realised he was aware of her scrutiny. 'How did you manage to acquire such a tan? With your colouring I would have thought you would burn quicker than me.'

He shrugged dismissively, his expression already settling back into more familiar lines. 'I used to have trouble when I was younger, but years of working outdoors on construction sites soon toughened me up. Now I have no problem in that area, but you'd be well advised to be extra careful while you're here. The Florida sun can be strong enough to cause real problems for people who don't respect its power.'

He turned as Jessica came rushing into the kitchen, a can of spray in her hands. Taking it from the child, he took the top off, then paused when she suddenly spoke.

'Can I go and see the foal, Daddy?'

He nodded briefly. 'Yes, but you aren't to go into the stable. Understand? Go find Frank and ask him to take you over. Tell him I said that I'd be across in a few minutes.'

Jessica nodded, then rushed out of the door, leaving it hanging open. Logan turned back to the task, shaking the spray before gently catching hold of Stephanie's hand.

'I can do it,' she said hurriedly. 'You carry on with your jobs.'

'I have time to spare a couple of minutes, and it's always difficult to treat your right hand with your left when you're right-handed.'

It was hard to dispute his logic, even harder to dispel the instant tension as he firmed his grip on her hand and covered the burn with a liberal coating of spray. He set the can down on the worktop, then ran a glance across the skin. 'That should do it. By tomorrow you shouldn't be able to feel a thing, but let me——'

'Logan, are you there?'

Stephanie recognised Cade Rylance's voice just an instant before the man appeared in the open door. She smiled at him, then became embarrassingly aware of the way his eyes had fallen to her hand, still held in Logan's. Hurriedly she tried to ease her fingers free, but surprisingly Logan seemed in no hurry to let her go. He glanced round at the other man, a faint brusqueness in his gravelly tones. 'Did you want me for something?'

Cade nodded. 'About those figures for the sales. I need to know how high you're prepared to go. There's a couple of excellent mares on offer, but they won't come cheap.'

'Then we'd better run through the catalogue.' Only then did he let Stephanie go, moving unhurriedly away from her as he walked out of the door. Cade Rylance lingered for a moment, faint curiosity on his face, before he tipped his hat to Stephanie and followed.

Stephanie leant back against the edge of the worktop, feeling suddenly weak-kneed at the strangeness of that little episode. Had she imagined it, or had there been just the faintest hint of warning in the way that Logan had kept hold of her hand, as though he was silently telling Cade Rylance that she was his property and to stay away?

She ran the idea through her mind several times, then slowly came to her senses. If there had been, then she knew the reason for it, and it owed little to any personal feelings Logan might have about her. He had been ensuring that Cade kept his distance to guarantee that both his manager and she performed their jobs to the standard he expected of them. That was the only thing the man cared about... nothing else!

That first day set the pattern for all the others that followed, so that a week slipped past before Stephanie realised it. Logan would spend a couple of hours early each morning around the farm and playing with Jessica, then would leave for his office. However, he always made sure that he was back on time, and there was no repeat of that first day's nightmares.

Under her attention, Jessica blossomed, losing most of the reserve that had been so apparent when Stephanie had first met her. She followed Stephanie around, hanging on to her every word, and Stephanie would have been a liar if she'd said that she didn't enjoy the adoration the child showed her. However, in some ways it did worry her.

Jessica was too young too spend all her time in the company of an adult. She needed other children to play with, fresh relationships that would make her less dependent. At the back of Stephanie's mind there was always the thought that she was only here for a matter of weeks and after that Jessica would have to adapt to someone new looking after her. If she had made some friends, then it would surely help cushion the blow.

Trying to find time to discuss her views with Logan without Jessica being present proved to be a problem. As soon as Jessica went to bed each night he would shut himself in the study with a deliberation that made Stephanie loath to disturb him. She was still smarting from those warnings he'd given about her not trying to make herself a permanent part of his life, and there was no way that she wanted him repeating them!

She voiced her concerns to Mary one morning when they were in the kitchen having a much needed cup of coffee. Frank's wife came in three times a weak to clean the large house and top up the groceries, and she and Stephanie had fast become friends. A pleasant, gentle woman, a bit older than Stephanie and mother of twin sons, she listened carefully before making a tentative suggestion of her own. 'I don't know what you think of the idea, but Jessica is always welcome to come and play with the boys. They're a year or so older than she is, and typical boys, a bit rough at times, but they're good-hearted. I'm sure they'd make her feel welcome.'

Stephanie smiled. 'That sounds marvellous! Why didn't I think of that? How about this afternoon?'

Mary nodded, but there was a trace of uncertainty on her face. 'It's fine by me, but do you think you should ask Mr Ford first? He might not like the idea of his daughter mixing with the farm children.'

Stephanie bristled at once. 'I don't see why! Leave Logan to me, Mary. I shall soon sort this out.'

'Mmm, I can see why there's been some speculation about your being here. You don't act like an employee, Stephanie!'

It was just gentle teasing, kindly meant and containing not a trace of malice, but Stephanie blushed furiously. Standing up, she snatched the cups off the table and carried them across to the sink, rinsing them more thoroughly than they merited. 'I *am* only an employee, Mary. You tell that to anyone who tries to tell you different. Logan Ford doesn't give me a second thought as long as Jessica is happy.'

'And how about you, honey? Do you give him a *second* thought? I'm happily married and wouldn't swap my Frank for anyone, but I'm still a woman. Frankly, there isn't a woman born who wouldn't give that man a second and maybe third thought!' She laughed softly, leaving Stephanie scrubbing furiously at the cup as though she were trying to erase the pattern of poppies from it.

With a sigh she set it down on the drainer and wiped her hands, feeling the faint roughness of her skin from where the burn had healed. Slowly her fingers traced over the patch as her mind spun back to how it had felt when Logan had done just the same thing—held her hand and smoothed the skin—and a faint insistent ache arose inside her. Mary was right; she did give Logan second thoughts, and third and fourth...! Far too many thoughts, in fact, especially when she knew he wouldn't thank her for them.

She was glad of Mary's offer later. The day had turned out to be blisteringly hot, too hot to play outside or swim in the pool. Jessica had grown increasingly restless, grumbling when Stephanie had insisted she should stay out of the sun. It was cool in the house, thanks to the efficient air-conditioning system, but it was no fun for the child to be cooped up. When Stephanie suggested that she might like to go over to Mary's house to play with her sons, the child displayed a mixture of eagerness at the idea of a change and a trace of uncertainty.

However, once Stephanie had taken her across to Mary's house in its neat little garden several hundred yards away from the main house, she soon forgot her fears in the excitement of having other children to play with. Greg and Craig were two nice boys, but they wouldn't treat Jessica any differently from their other school friends. Stephanie was glad, because she had the idea that Jessica hadn't been allowed to mix much in the past with other children. A touch of rough and tumble would do her good, knock some of the corners off her and allow her to fit in better when she started back at school. She could only speculate on what sort of a life the child had led, but the fact that she'd been left to the care of her grandmother and Teresa a lot of the time couldn't be healthy.

Stephanie was lost in thought about how to broach the subject of Jessica's grandmother to Logan as she waved goodbye to the children after promising to collect Jessica in an hour. She'd had no opportunity to talk to him about the situation, but something needed to be done about it. Unconsciously her mouth thinned as a possible scenario flashed into her mind, Logan standing there, haughty and arrogant, telling her to mind her own business. Well, this was her business! She was here to look after Jessica's welfare, and seeing her grandmother was crucial to that.

'My, my, I'd hate to be on the receiving end of those thoughts! Something bothering you, Stephanie?'

Cade Rylance's softly amused voice drew her attention to the fact that she'd almost walked past him. She stopped at once, shading her eyes as she looked up at him, and grinned. 'Just thank heavens they're all reserved for our boss.'

He grinned, tightening his hold on the lead rope of the huge chestnut horse he was taking back towards the paddocks. 'So what's he done now to annoy you?'

She shrugged, pushing her hands deep into the pockets of her white shorts as she leant against the rail and stared across the green field. 'Nothing more than he normally does.' She sighed suddenly, a faintly wistful expression in her eyes that she was unaware of. 'That's unfair, I suppose. He's done nothing really. I'm just a bit concerned about the way he's cut Jessica off from her grandmother. It doesn't make sense.'

Cade ran a hand down the chestnut's nose, soothing its increasingly restless tugging on the lead rope. 'It probably would if you knew all the background to it.'

'Maybe, but I don't... unless you're offering to tell me?'

The man shook his head, his face closing. 'Sorry, but that's for Logan to tell you about, not me. He wouldn't thank me for talking about his past.'

'I'm glad you realise that, Cade.'

She'd had no warning of his approach, too caught up with her own thoughts and wondering what the mystery was in Logan's past. Now Stephanie whirled round with a startled cry as she recognised his voice. The horse shied violently at her sudden movement, its ears flattening against its head, its nostrils flaring. It reared up on its hind legs, hoofs flailing wildly. Cade shouted something but she didn't catch it, frozen in place by surprise. Something caught her round the waist, iron bands that crushed the breath from her body as she was lifted out of the way just a second before the horse's hoofs came back down, hitting the spot where she'd been standing.

Stephanie shuddered, closing her eyes, feeling the iciness of fear and shock seeping into her bones. Unconsciously she burrowed deeper into the hard warmth she was resting against, feeling shaken to the core by her narrow escape. When Logan's voice rumbled almost in her ear she started nervously at the white-hot anger she could hear burning in the harsh tones, missing Cade's response as he led the horse away.

'Are you all right? It didn't hit you, just gave you a scare.'

She'd never fully realised before how delicious that gravelly voice could sound when it gentled as it had done now. Ripples of sensation ran along her raw nerves, smoothing and soothing before setting up a chain reaction of heat coursing through her cold body to chase away the lingering chills of fear. Stephanie smiled faintly, letting herself nestle a moment longer against the solid strength of Logan's broad chest, breathing in the heady scent of his skin, feeling the heavy beat of his heart pressing against the softness of her breast. 'I'm fine...honestly, Logan.'

'Good.' With a quick lift of his hands he set her away from him, his big hands biting into her shoulders as he glared down into her startled face. 'Then would you mind telling me what the hell you were up to?' He shook her, not hard, not roughly, but enough to make her feel almost like a limp little rag. 'You're supposed to be taking care of my daughter, not entertaining my manager. Where is she?'

Stephanie blinked up at him, her reeling senses stealing her ability to speak. He swore roughly, a string of colourful oaths that brought the colour into her face, and she pulled herself away from him. 'Do you mind?'

'No, frankly. Now I asked you a question, so how about an answer? Where is Jessica, and what has she been doing while you've been...busy?'

He laid an unpleasant emphasis on the last word, but Stephanie refused to dignify the implied accusation by answering it. She stared back at him, blue eyes meeting brown with as much disdain as she could muster. 'She's over at Mary's house, playing with the twins.'

'So that's what goes on when I'm not here, is it? You off-load your responsibilities on to someone else?' His anger was so great now that she had the sudden craziest idea that she could have burned herself if she'd touched him. It was totally unjust, of course, but before she could even begin to set him straight he continued, 'Well, Miss Stephanie Jacobs, I think this is where our agreement ends, don't you? If you imagine that I'm putting up with this kind of behaviour, then think again. I want you to get your things together and be ready to leave within half an hour!'

He turned to stride back to the house, leaving Stephanie staring after him in open-mouthed horror. He couldn't mean it; he really couldn't mean that he was *sacking* her for something she hadn't even done!

She started after him, calling his name, but he ignored her as he carried on walking, his long legs eating up the ground. Stephanie broke into a run, perspiration breaking out all over her body as she raced after him, but he was almost at the steps leading on to the back porch before she caught up with him. Flushed and breathless, she caught his arm and tried to swing him round, but he was far too strong for her to do that. He merely slowed, staring at her with cold black eyes that glimmered with contempt.

'I don't think we have anything left to say, Stephanie.'

If only she was six feet three and weighed fifteen stone, then she would have taken great pleasure in wiping that expression off his lordly face! Gulping in a lungful of much needed air, she clung to his arm and faced him defiantly. 'Perhaps *you* don't have anything to say, Mr Ford, but *I* do! And for starters you are entirely out of line accusing me of what you just have. I met Cade by accident. It wasn't some sort of tryst we'd made! Nor did I off-load my responsibilities about Jessica!'

'I hardly expected you to admit it. Half an hour, Stephanie. If your bags aren't packed and downstairs by then I shall pack them for you!'

'And what about Jessica? How do you think she's going to react to the fact I'm being forced to leave? Who is going to take care of her?' There was a note of desperation in her voice, but he ignored it as he stared levelly at her.

'It's rather late in the day to start worrying about her, isn't it?' he said icily. 'But don't concern yourself too much. My daughter won't suffer, even if I have to make arrangements to work from home until I can find someone suitable to look after her. I think I prefer the inconvenience of that and all the undoubted problems it will bring to putting up with what has been going on behind my back!'

He drew his arm away and carried on into the house. Stephanie watched him go with a lump of pain in her heart. She didn't want to leave. She wanted to stay and take care of Jessica and...

Her mind closed off the thought, but it couldn't be held at bay for long. It seeped past all the barriers she tried to erect, flowing through every pore in her body to fill her with a sense of such futility that tears ran down her face. She wanted to stay and take care of Jessica... and remain as close to Logan as she could. He might not want *her* in his life, but she wanted to be in *his*, and it was only now when it was too late that she fully understood how much.

CHAPTER SEVEN

THE suitcase was a mess. Stephanie stared down at the jumble of clothes through a veil of tears, then took a shuddering little breath as she snapped the locks. Lifting the case off the bed, she took a last look around the room, then walked towards the door.

'I see you're ready.' Logan came into the room, his face betraying nothing as he took the case from her, and Stephanie choked back a sob. Without a word she followed him downstairs, her head bowed so that he wouldn't see her tears. She should feel angry at the way he was treating her, but this wasn't anger, just a sense of utter desolation.

'Have you got everything? You haven't left anything in the sitting-room or the kitchen?' There was no give in those harsh tones, and any thoughts she might have had about asking him to reconsider died abruptly. She wouldn't beg. She wouldn't debase herself that much. She would hold on to her pride, because that was all she had.

She raised her head and stared defiantly back at him. 'I haven't left anything. Don't worry. Once you've got rid of me today, then I won't be back. You can be sure of that!'

His mouth thinned. 'Good. I don't want to see hide nor hair of you ever again, Stephanie. Am I making myself clear? So if you had any ideas of coming back here to visit Rylance, then I suggest that you——'

'Daddy! You're home early... Why is Stephanie's case down here?' Jessica burst through the door, her smile fading as she took in the scene. Behind her Stephanie saw Mary pause uncertainly in the doorway, but after a murmured apology the other woman left.

'Stephie? You aren't leaving, are you?' Jessica's voice rose, her face puckering as tears ran down her face. She raced across the hall and grasped hold of Stephanie's hand. 'You can't go! I don't want you to. I want you to stay here. Tell her, Daddy. Tell her to stay!'

The child turned beseechingly to Logan, but he merely set the case down then went and drew her away from Stephanie. 'Stephanie has to leave, Jess. I know you're sad to see her go and that you will miss her for a while, but I shall find someone else to look after you. Until I do, I shall try to work at home as much as I can to be with you.'

'I don't want anyone else! I want Stephanie. I love her!' Dragging herself free, Jessica hurtled back to wrap her arms around Stephanie's waist, her small body shuddering with sobs. Stephanie dropped to her knees, unaware that tears were streaming down her own face as she held the child close.

'Don't cry like that, poppet. You'll make yourself sick. Daddy will find someone nice to take care of you.'

Jessica rubbed her wet face with the back of her hand. 'I don't want anyone but you... ever! Why do you want to go, Stephie? Don't you love me too?'

'Of course I do.' She kissed the flushed wet cheek, feeling the sense of loss growing even bigger. 'If I ever have a little girl then I hope she will be just like you, Jessica.'

'Then why go? Stay with me, please.'

'I can't, love. I just can't.'

'Why not?' Jessica stared into Stephanie's face, seeking an answer that it was impossible to give her. Stephanie looked away, glancing helplessly up at Logan as she wondered how to explain that she wasn't going for reasons of her own. If she told Jessica the truth—that it was Logan who wanted her to leave—then she could only speculate on the damage it could cause. Jessica was still so vulnerable after the death of her mother; she needed Logan, needed to know that he cared about her. There was no way that Stephanie would risk damaging their relationship just to get back at Logan.

There was a moment's deep, intense silence, as though all of them were trying to work out what to do next, then Logan spoke, instantly claiming their attention. 'Perhaps Stephanie will agree to stay if I ask her as well, Jess.'

Jessica turned to look at him, relief glowing in her eyes. 'Will you do that, Daddy?'

Logan glanced at Stephanie, his dark eyes hooded. 'Yes.' He walked towards them, offering Stephanie his hand as Jessica moved away from her. Stephanie hesitated, somehow loath to touch those long, strong fingers in case this was some sort of cruel trick that Logan was playing on her, but he just said quietly, 'Will you stay, Stephanie? Please.'

As an apology it should have rated next to nothing; as an apology from *Logan* it meant far more than that. Slowly she slipped her fingers into his, feeling the strength of his grip as he helped her up, before he let her hand go and studied her with a question in his eyes. Stephanie took a long, shuddering breath, wondering if she was being a fool. If she agreed to stay, then how much more painful would it be in a few weeks' time when she really did have to go? She'd have had that much more time to grow increasingly attached to Jessica...that much more time to fall in love with Logan!

The shock must have shown on her face, because Logan muttered something rough under his breath as he took a hurried step towards her. Stephanie held up her hand to ward him off, terrified of letting him touch her in case she fell apart in front of him. 'I'm all right. Just a bit dizzy with getting up, I expect.' Her voice was hoarse, rasping with tension as she tried to blank the disturbing thought from her mind. She wasn't about to fall in love with Logan...she wasn't! She wouldn't allow herself to commit such an act of folly.

'You are going to stay, Stephie, aren't you?' Jessica broke the silence as she caught Stephanie's hand and stared worriedly up at her. Stephanie forced a smile to lips that felt as though they'd been carved from stone.

'Yes, if you're both sure that's what you want.' She spoke to Jessica, but she and Logan both knew who the question was directed at.

'It is what we want, Stephanie,' he replied quietly. He picked up her case and carried it back up the stairs without another word. Stephanie watched him, a pain so intense burning in her heart that it felt as though an unseen hand were tearing it to shreds. Even to the last Logan was unbending. He'd only changed his mind about her staying for his daughter's sake, and she must never, ever forget that.

She was sitting on the porch, watching Jessica swimming in the pool, when Logan suddenly appeared. She'd not seen him since he'd carried her case back upstairs, and now she could feel slow colour burning her face as she looked up and found him watching her. Shading her eyes against the glare from the late afternoon sun, she deliberately ignored him, but she could feel her heart starting to beat furiously when she heard his slow footsteps coming towards her.

He stopped beside her chair, leaning back against the porch rail as he continued to study her in that disturbing way. Stephanie shifted uneasily, still refusing to look at him, and heard him sigh with rough impatience.

'We're going to have to make an effort to forget what happened today for Jessica's sake.'

'I doubt it will be that easy, Logan, do you?' She looked at him at last, studying the set lines of his strong face, the shuttered expression in those dark-chocolate eyes, and bit back a sigh. 'You made some dreadful accusations before. You were way out of line, and we both know it.'

'Do we? Just because I asked you to stay doesn't mean that I take back what I said to you. You had no right off-loading your responsibility for Jessica on to someone else!'

The sheer nerve of the man. Who did he think he was? Some divine being who knew everything? She came to her feet in a rush and glared back at him. 'If that's your attitude, Logan, then I think I'd better go and pack my case again!'

He stepped in front of her as she started back inside the house, his face set into grim lines. 'You're not going anywhere. We're going to talk this through so that you know exactly where your duties lie in future. I may have been willing to give you a second chance this time, but I won't give you a third.'

'*We* are going to talk this through?' She laughed scornfully, throwing the words straight back into his arrogant face. 'Don't you mean that you are going to talk and that I am going to listen? Sorry, Logan, that might be the way you do business with other people, but you are not pushing me around. So I suggest you think about that, then maybe you and I can talk!'

She stepped around him, head high as she headed for the door, then stopped uncertainly when she heard the soft sound of his laugh. She glanced back in surprise, then felt a prickle of heat touch her spine when she saw not anger on his handsome face but a reluctant admiration.

He came towards her, stopping just a foot away as he leant a shoulder against the house wall and stared straight back at her with just the barest lift of one dark brow. 'Well, I'd better hear it, then, hadn't I?'

'What? Hear what?' She wasn't proof against his closeness, the heat of his big body, the faintly spicy smell of soap and man. It made her senses stir with awareness, and angered her at once!

He must have seen the glint in her blue eyes, because he glanced over his shoulder at the child playing happily in the pool before taking Stephanie's arm and leading her into the coolness of the hall. 'I think we'd be better talking about this out of Jessica's hearing. Come in here.'

He ushered her into the huge sitting-room with its pale cream carpeting and soft green upholstery. It was a beautiful room, elegant yet comfortable, the windows at either end giving it an airy feel even on the hottest day. Walking across to the window that overlooked the pool at the back of the house, Logan stood with his back to Stephanie as he watched his daughter splashing happily in the water. 'Obviously you disagree with my assessment of the situation, so why not tell me your side of it?'

Did he *really* want to hear it, or was it just some sort of a sop to stop her from arguing and upsetting Jessica further? There was no way of knowing, so as briefly as possible Stephanie outlined the reasons why she had taken Jessica to Mary's house to play with the boys. She stared fixedly at Logan's broad back, wishing he would turn round so that she could see his face, then realised just how foolish a wish that was. If he didn't want her to know what he thought, then he would have little difficulty in hiding his feelings from her!

'That's the only reason I had for taking her to play there. You can believe me or not, that's your privilege, but surely even you can see that Jessica needs other children to play with?'

He turned as she finally stopped speaking, his shoulders hunching as he rammed his hands in the pockets of his trousers. He was still wearing his business clothes, although he'd shed the jacket of the elegant navy pin-striped suit that fit his muscular frame to perfection, and he looked every inch the tough boss of a multi-million-dollar corporation. Stephanie felt her heart sink as she wondered why she'd bothered wasting her breath explaining. He was bound not to believe her, bound to think that he was right!

'That damned horse could have killed you!'

'Pardon?' She jumped at the harsh statement, staring at him in confusion before she drew her thoughts back into some sort of order. 'Perhaps it could have, but it didn't, so there isn't any point in dwelling on it, I don't suppose.'

'Maybe not, but it just serves to emphasise a point, and that is that it would never have happened if you'd been attending to your own business and steered clear of Rylance!'

Did he really think she was going to let him get away with that? He must do, but was he in for a surprise. She marched towards him, glaring coldly into his set face. 'For your information, Logan, I happened to meet Cade by accident. And if you hadn't come pussyfooting up on us, hoping to discover some sort of sordid intimate secrets, then none of this would have happened. You startled me, I startled the horse, and bingo!'

'So you are saying that what nearly happened was my fault?'

'Too right! I've explained to you about Jessica, and even you must agree that what I say is right: she does need to play with other children. Maybe now you can accept that I'm telling you the truth about my meeting with Cade—not that I need to explain that to you. You don't own me, Logan Ford. Understand? Now if you have finished with the Spanish Inquisition you're running here...' She half turned to walk away, vaguely pleased by the way she'd put him firmly in his place, but her pleasure was short-lived as he stepped in front of her to bar her way.

'So you find my manager attractive, do you, honey?' There was just something about the way he said that, the faint emphasis he placed on the word 'manager' so that there was a slightly derogatory ring to it. Stephanie stiffened at once; Cade Rylance had been nothing but polite to her since she'd arrived, and there was no way she was going to let the man be insulted because of his kindness to her!

'Of course. Which woman wouldn't find him attractive?' She forced a slow, seductive little laugh, enjoying the way Logan's brows lowered and his eyes glittered dangerously. There was something exciting about pushing him this way, taking the tension and twisting it out thinner and thinner until it was about to snap. 'He's a very handsome man, and add to that his beautiful manners, that innate courtesy of his, and you end up with a very attractive package.'

'I see. So what you are trying to say, Stephanie, is that you find him... desirable? He makes you aware of him, sets off sparks, does he?'

She didn't like the way his voice had dropped to a low growl, nor the way he moved a deliberate step closer to her as he stared into her eyes, then let his gaze drop to her mouth. Unconsciously her lips parted, a tiny breath sighing out between them, her whole body suddenly going rigid as the fragile link snapped, leaving her teetering on the very edge of some unseen precipice.

When he reached out to smooth a wisp of hair behind her ear, she jerked helplessly, her eyes widening as they met his and read the message they contained. 'Don't...do...that!' she ordered hoarsely.

He smiled slowly. 'Don't do...what? This?' Once again he reached out to smooth her hair, twining one long silky strand around his index finger and tugging gently on the curl so that her head moved a fraction closer to him. He held her there for a heartbeat, then slowly unravelled the shining strands and brushed them away from her face, his fingers touching so gently against her cheek that she shivered. 'Is this how Cade makes you feel, honey? So aware of him that you ache?'

'I... No! I mean, that's none of your damn business!' She pushed him away, wrapping her arms tightly around herself to stop the shudders that were pulsing through her body.

'Normally I would agree with you... it isn't any of my business... but while you're here it is.' He stared levelly at her, his voice once more harsh and unyielding. Had she imagined what had just happened? She didn't think so, didn't think she was capable of imagining the sensations that he'd brought to life with just a few brief touches. She swallowed hard, her mouth so dry that it was difficult to speak as she fought against the lingering waves of heat and desire that lay curled in the pit of her stomach.

'Don't worry, Logan. My only concern while I'm here is Jessica.'

'I'm pleased to hear it. Glad too that we've managed to get a few things sorted out between us.' There was a faint satisfaction on his face as he studied the betraying tension in her stance, and Stephanie felt herself colour. He was too experienced with women to not understand how she felt, too aware of his own sexuality and the effect it could have. He'd set out to teach her a lesson and he had, but why? Why should he want to make her admit to herself that it was he who had this strange effect on her senses, not his manager?

She frowned as she tried to work it out, but before she could find an answer he continued speaking. 'I shall be going out tonight. That's partly the reason why I came home so early today. I wanted to spend some time with Jessica before I have to leave. In fact I think I'll go and join her in the pool for a while.'

He started walking towards the door, then stopped as he felt in his pocket and drew out a slip of paper and laid it down on the table beside the sofa. 'That's the number where you can get me if you need to.'

Stephanie went and picked it up, more out of a desire to put it somewhere safe than any other reason. Incuriously she glanced down at the name and number, then raised her head with a faint gasp of shock.

Logan smiled faintly, his eyes skimming her face. 'You remember Melissa, don't you? We met her in Orlando. She's offered to cook me a special meal.' He laughed deeply. 'Funny, but she didn't strike me as a domesticated woman at all!'

When Stephanie made no response he carried on towards the door, then paused once more to glance back at where she was still standing as though frozen to the spot. 'And by the way, honey... don't wait up for me. I could be late!'

Why of all the... Snatching up one of the silk-covered cushions off the sofa, Stephanie hurled it after him, watching angrily as it landed harmlessly in the empty doorway. If he imagined that she cared one way or the other whom he dated or how long he intended to stay, he was mistaken. He could stay the night with Melissa Cooper, or all week or all damned year! It didn't matter to her what he did!

She went and retrieved the cushion, clutching it tightly to her chest as she closed her eyes and admitted that it was all lies. She *did* care what Logan did and with whom. She cared far too much, and there was no point in pretending otherwise and storing up more trouble for herself. She had to face up to the feelings growing inside her, not pretend they didn't exist. Maybe in that way when it was time to leave Florida she wouldn't end up by leaving her heart behind.

She didn't intend to be up when Logan returned. She'd gone to bed shortly before ten and taken a bath to help her to unwind, but sleep just wouldn't come. First she was too hot, then too cold after she'd turned the air-conditioning up, and then she was beset by a raging thirst.

Muttering crossly to herself, Stephanie pulled on her silky pink robe and padded barefoot down to the kitchen to get a drink. She didn't bother with the main light, just switched on the strip light under the cupboards as she filled a glass with chilled fruit juice, then on a sudden impulse unlocked the back door and carried it out to the porch.

The night was warm and quiet, a faint breeze barely rustling the leaves on the huge oak tree that stood just beyond the steps to the porch. Stephanie took a sip of the juice, then closed her eyes as she let the peace sink into her tired mind to soothe away all the thoughts that would keep on filling it. It took the sound of a car engine and the gleam of headlights coming towards the house to rouse her, but not fast enough for her to escape back inside before Logan drew up outside.

He climbed out and came towards her, one dark brow inching upwards as he studied her standing there, and Stephanie felt her temper start to rise, fuelled by the embarrassment of the situation.

'I was thirsty, so I came down to get a drink.'

'I see.' It was the way he said that, with such complete disbelief, that tipped her over the edge.

'I don't think you do! I was *not* waiting up to check on you, Logan. Understand now?'

He merely nodded, walking up the steps as he shrugged off his beige jacket and draped it carelessly over one of the porch chairs. With it he wore a short-sleeved cream shirt and taupe trousers that moulded his long legs as he sat down and stretched them out in front of him. In the dim half-light spilling from the open doorway his hair looked rich and vibrant, his skin gleaming with a golden tan. He looked so incredibly handsome and so undeniably male that Stephanie felt her pulse skip a beat before racing wildly.

Hurriedly she raised the glass to her lips and took a drink of the cool liquid, wishing he would say something, but it was several tense seconds before he replied to her hasty denial.

'Pity. I think most men would appreciate having you waiting up for them, especially dressed in that very fetching outfit.' His eyes did a lazy assessment of her slender body in the clinging pink robe, making her suddenly achingly conscious of the thinness of the material and of the short matching gown she wore underneath. Unconsciously she drew the folds around her, avoiding looking directly at him, yet she could feel the heat of his gaze in a way that made her whole body ache and her nipples tauten in a sudden undeniable reaction she could only pray he didn't notice.

With a shaking hand she set the glass down on the white wicker table and smiled tightly at a point somewhere to the right of his head. 'Don't tell me that was actually a compliment, Logan. My, my, but you must have had a good evening to soften that much!'

He laughed softly, leaning back comfortably in the chair as he continued his lazy scrutiny. 'I'm beginning to see that I was a bit over-optimistic about our relationship, Stephanie. It isn't easy to ignore you, is it? Not when you're always so ready to jump back at me and make those sparks ignite.'

The words brought back all too vividly their earlier conversation, and she couldn't help the hot blush that ran up her cheeks. She glared down at him, knowing without the shadow of a doubt that he'd said that deliberately to remind her of what had gone on. 'I don't think that there's any reason to continue along that track, Logan. I think you're in danger of going for overkill on that topic.'

'I disagree. I always think it pays to face facts, and the simple fact is that there are sparks when you and I get together, Stephanie...for whatever reason.' He stood up suddenly, his smile deepening as she started nervously. 'Would you like another drink? I think I'll join you.'

She shook her head as she inched towards the door, not liking the way the conversation was moving. 'Er—no, thank you. I think it's time I went back to bed.'

'Not running away, are you, honey? That doesn't seem quite your style.'

'I have no idea what you mean. I'm simply going back to bed.'

'What's the rush? It's a beautiful night, so why not enjoy it?' He rested an arm against the door-frame, muscles rippling as he took his weight on it and studied her face. Stephanie swallowed hard, not wanting to let him think that she was afraid of him in any way, yet all too aware of the danger in staying here with him in this strangely unsettling mood.

'I'll take it that means you'll stay for a while.' He picked up her glass and carried it back inside, reappearing a minute or two later with it refilled and another one for himself. He set them down on the table, then waited until she'd reluctantly sat down on one of the deeply padded chairs before sitting next to her. Stephanie picked up the glass but barely wet her lips with the juice as she searched for some safe topic to break the increasingly intimate silence. It was so peaceful outside, the sky like velvet above their heads, the faint light just illuminating this small area of the porch. It felt as though they were the only two people left in the world, locked into their own small space.

'How was Jessica tonight? Did she settle down all right?'

It was a relief to hear him speak on such a safe topic. Stephanie relaxed slightly, settling back in the chair as she smiled faintly. 'Yes. There were no problems at all about that. I think she was tired out with all the excitement of playing with Mary's boys.'

'Good.' He picked up his glass and took a swallow, staring into the distance. 'I wish I'd realised she needed other children's company. I should have done, but...' He shrugged, but there was a note of self-condemnation in his voice that made Stephanie hurry to reassure him.

'You probably would have done in time. Don't forget it's my job to deal with children and assess their needs; it's what I'm trained to do.'

'That isn't any excuse. I should have thought about it sooner.'

Silence fell again, a brooding silence that hummed with emotions that Stephanie could barely understand. Logan was being too hard on himself, but that was the type of man he was. He would aim for perfection in everything he did and settle for nothing less than the best, but it wasn't that simple when raising a child. There were so many things she would like to ask him about Jessica and Amanda and the life they'd all led, but she wasn't fool enough to think he would tell her. He considered that to be his business and nobody else's, but it didn't stop the question from filling her head.

Anxious to take her mind off it, she changed the subject and said the first thing that came into her head. 'So how was your evening? Did you have fun?'

She just managed to hold back the groan as she realised how that must sound, berating herself for being so stupid when she saw the mockery on his face.

'It was fine. Thank you for asking, Stephanie. Melissa is an extremely charming and sophisticated woman.'

Did he need to be quite so effusive? He wasn't supposed to be providing Melissa Cooper with a reference, for heaven's sake, just replying to a simple, polite question. Annoyance rippled through her as she pondered on what exactly the woman had done to earn such praise. Obviously the beautiful Melissa had made an impression, but had she actually managed to pierce that armour he wore to shield his emotions? Indeed, was there any woman who could do that?

She wasn't aware of how betraying her expression was until he leant forwards and turned her face to his as he studied her with narrowed eyes. 'Now what is going on inside that pretty head, I wonder? I wish I had a dollar for every one of those obviously disturbing thoughts, sweet Stephanie.'

There was a glint in his eyes that demanded that she answer him truthfully, but there was no way she was going to do that. She moved her head so that his hand dropped away. 'I doubt you'd earn yourself a fortune. I'm tired, that's all. It's been a long and eventful day.'

'It has.' There was a sudden edge to his voice. 'Why did you agree to stay on? It's something we never touched on before.'

'I...' She searched for the right words, afraid of saying something too revealing. 'Jessica obviously wanted me to.'

'And that was the only reason?'

'Of course. What other could I have? It was you who told me to go, Logan. It wasn't my choice. So why did you ask me to stay?'

'Because I realised I had underestimated Jessica's reaction to your going.' He shrugged slightly. 'I'll do anything in my power to help her through this rough patch. I've consulted several child specialists about the best way to handle what has happened to her, and accept what they say—that with the right care and love she will put it behind her. I just need to give her as much stability as possible to help the healing process.'

'So it was better to change your mind and ask me to stay for the next few weeks rather than upset her any more?' She smiled bitterly, suddenly understanding the reason behind the conversation. 'Don't worry, Logan. I understand perfectly.'

'Do you?'

'Yes!' She stood up abruptly. There was a huge weight in her heart, but she refused to think about the reason for it. Logan had made his meaning very clear and left her in no doubt as to why he had changed his mind. She started back into the kitchen, then paused to turn back for her glass, unaware that Logan had stood up also, so that she cannoned into him. Instinctively her hands came up, although whether to steady herself or to ward him off she wasn't sure.

Her fingers brushed across his chest, barely touching the hard muscles, yet she was left reeling from the sensation of heat and strength which seemed to steal her ability to move. Her hands lingered on the thin cotton, and as she watched something started to burn in his eyes. He pulled her abruptly to him, holding her so close that she could feel every line of his powerful body through the thinness of her night clothes.

'No, Logan! Don't.' She could barely speak, let alone order him to stop, and he smiled arrogantly, correctly interpreting the mixed signals coming from her body. He drew her even closer, one hand dropping to the hollow of her back while the other slid into her silky hair as he burrowed his fingers through the long strands.

'Why not? It's what you want.' He bent and brushed her mouth with his, teasing her with the most fleeting of kisses that made a slow curl of fire lick along her veins, before he drew back and studied her face.

'You're wrong. I don't want this! I don't——' His mouth silenced the rest of her protests as he kissed her again with a slow, deliberate seduction that fanned the fire into a conflagration. Stephanie moaned a protest, twisting her head against his hold, but he merely twined her hair around his fingers so that it became too painful to resist. Mentally she fought the kiss, steeled herself against the drugging assault on her senses, but by the time he raised his head again she was shaking from the effort it cost her.

'And you really imagine that Rylance could have this sort of effect on you, honey?' He laughed harshly, a thin line of colour etched along his angular cheekbones. 'He's too much of a gentleman for you. You need a man with fire to match your own!'

She had to make him stop before this got completely out of control. 'Fire? Then that lets you out, Logan. You're ice, through and through!'

'Is that a fact?' He brought his hand round to run his thumb across her swollen lips, inching the lower one down a fraction so that she could feel the abrasive roughness against the soft inner flesh in a touch that made her shudder with reaction. He felt it at once, of course, felt the helpless, betraying tremble that ran through her limbs. His hand splayed across her back, each finger leaving its burning imprint through the robe as he smiled with deep satisfaction.

'Perhaps I am ice, but you and I both know that I can light fires inside you. Doesn't it tempt you to see if you can make me melt?'

'No! No...no...no!' She started to struggle, something about the way he was looking at her making her afraid, although not of what he might do but of her own response. Logan *did* light fires inside her, but she wasn't fool enough to want to take him up on that offer.

When he kissed her for a third time, she clamped her mouth tightly shut and went rigid in his arms, praying that would stop the game he was playing, but he was too experienced for that. Instead of trying to force her, his mouth gentled, tender, fleeting kisses brushing back and forth across her lips, teasing and tormenting, inviting a response she didn't want to give.

With a sheer effort of will, Stephanie tried to block the sensations from her mind, but when his tongue suddenly traced a delicate foray across her lips she was lost. Her helpless gasp was swallowed up as he took advantage of it to let his tongue slide inside her mouth, and the last of her control shattered into a thousand pieces. She kissed him back, her hands smoothing across his chest as she learned the contours of it just as her tongue learned the sweet contours of his mouth.

When he started to set her from him, she clung, not wanting the kiss to end. Her whole body was throbbing with desire, aching with a primitive need for possession she'd never experienced before. How could Logan make her feel this way? And why?

It was just a faint whisper at the back of her mind, but it grew stronger as she felt those hands slowly pushing her away now, felt the heat of passion start to cool. Why had Logan kissed her like that when he'd been at great pains to make her understand he didn't want any sort of relationship other than that of employer and employee?

She stepped back from him abruptly, suddenly chilled by the questions she needed to hear answers to, but in the end Logan supplied them without her having to ask.

He ran a hand through his hair, smoothing a few dishevelled strands back from his forehead as he watched her in a way that made the last of the heat fade. 'It seems that I was right, Stephanie. I got to wondering this evening about why you'd agreed so readily to stay on, you see. I decided to make sure that you understood the position quite clearly so that there would be no future problems. I am a great believer in facing facts, and the simple fact is that you are attracted to me.' He paused for a moment, but Stephanie couldn't find the words to say, words that would disabuse him of that idea. What would be the point in lying about something they both knew now was the truth?

Shame filled her and she bowed her head, barely hearing him as he continued, 'I don't deny that I find you attractive, honey. Why lie? But the plain fact of the matter is that I don't intend that attraction to go any further than it has done tonight. Look on this as an exercise in common sense. We've discovered what it feels like to enjoy a few kisses, and removed the temptation that good old-fashioned curiosity always adds to a situation. It was pleasant while it lasted, but...' He shrugged dismissively, then walked around her to disappear inside the house.

Stephanie wrapped her arms tightly around her body, but it was impossible to stop the feeling that she was being torn apart as pain ripped through her. Pleasant! Was that the word to describe that magic, that hot surge of sensations she'd never experienced before in her life?

She took a choking breath and stumbled to the steps, sitting down as her legs gave way. Leaning her head against the white-painted post, she stared into the distance and wished she'd never heard of Florida and Logan Ford. People called this the sunshine state, but that was laughable. There wasn't enough sunshine in the whole of it to melt that man's frozen heart!

CHAPTER EIGHT

IT WAS impossible to put what had happened out of her mind. Stephanie found herself going over and over everything Logan had said, the ruthless way he had manipulated her. He never once alluded to it, of course. He had made his point and that was that as far as he was concerned, but it was always there in the back of her mind if not in his, putting an added strain on her dealings with him. How she envied him that cold ability to categorise his life. If she could do the same, slot Logan into the category of employer, then there would be no problem. But there was no way she could ever do that now.

From the few comments Mary made, Stephanie soon realised that rumours of their argument had spread. She did her best to brush them aside by making out that it had been a silly misunderstanding that had been worked out between them now. However, she couldn't help but notice that Cade Rylance seemed to make a point of keeping out of her way, and that saddened her. She had the feeling that the two of them could have become friends, but not now.

It would have been different, of course, if she could have explained why Logan had been so angry that day, but any explanations were just too embarrassing. She had the feeling that Logan's manager would soon read between the lines if she tried to make up some story. He was too perceptive not to realise he was hearing only part of the truth, too perceptive to miss how she was starting to feel about Logan, and she didn't want anyone guessing about that.

Once it became obvious that the upset had caused no lasting harm to Jessica, and that the child was settling down, Logan started working later each day. Stephanie had the feeling that there were some problems with his latest project, but she never enquired as to what they were. He was unfailingly polite whenever they spoke, but uncompromising in his determination to keep her firmly in her allotted role. He would deem any questions about his business as none of her concern.

Several times he phoned to say that he would be home late because he had a dinner engagement. Stephanie could only speculate on who his companion might be, but she had little doubt that it was Melissa Cooper. She tried to tell herself that she didn't care, but it was all lies, of course.

There was a little over a week left before she was due to leave. The weather had suddenly turned stormy, rain and wind lashing across the fields, although the heat was still oppressive. With Jessica playing at the twins' house, Stephanie was filling in time by making a half-hearted attempt to write to Rachel, and was glad of the interruption when the phone suddenly rang. Leaving the letter on the table, she hurried to answer it, unable to stop the involuntary shudder that ran through her when she recognised Logan's voice.

'I've left some papers on the desk in the study that I need urgently. Do you think you can go and find them for me, please?'

Typically he didn't bother wasting time on polite preliminaries, and Stephanie responded in kind, deliberately blanking her mind of any foolish thoughts that had no business there.

'Of course. Tell me what they are and I'll go and look for them.' She listened carefully, then hurried to the study, experiencing no difficulty in finding the papers where he'd said. Picking up the extension on the desk, she quietly told him that she had them.

'Good. I need them straight away. Something urgent has cropped up here, a query about the boundaries of the land.' His voice was rough with impatience. 'Get Frank to drive over with them at once. This can't wait. There's too much money at stake if those lawyers have made a mistake, and, believe me, heads will roll if I discover that they have!'

There was no mistaking his anger, and Stephanie felt a momentary sympathy for the person who might have made the error that was short-lived as she suddenly realised she couldn't carry out his instructions.

'Logan...wait!' He'd already started to cut the connection without bothering to say goodbye. Stephanie clamped down on the fruitless stab of pain, realising that as far as Logan was concerned there'd been no need to waste time on meaningless niceties.

'Yes? What is it? If you have a problem, Stephanie, I'm sure it can wait until tonight when I get back.'

'You mean you're actually gracing us with your presence tonight? We are honoured.' She hadn't meant to say that, especially not in that tone. She closed her eyes and prayed that he hadn't heard what she had in her voice, but she was a fool to imagine that Logan would miss something so revealing.

'Careful, honey, your jealousy is starting to show.'

His voice was deep, grating along every fibre of her body in a way she bitterly resented. Deliberately she whipped up her anger, using it to hide how she really felt. 'Don't kid yourself, Logan! It will be a cold day in hell when I'm ever jealous of you.'

'While I'd love to debate that point with you, I'm afraid I don't have time. So either tell me what's bothering you or leave it until later.'

He sounded bored now and impatient, as though talking to her was just a waste of his precious time, and suddenly all her anger faded in the face of futility. Logan cared nothing about how she felt; he never had and he never would.

'It can't wait.' Her voice was flat and emotionless now. It obviously bothered him in some way, because there was a faint hesitation now when he replied.

'Then you'd better tell me what it is. There's nothing wrong with Jess, is there?'

'No, of course not. She's over at Mary's, playing with the twins. But there is a problem with getting these papers to you. Frank has gone with Cade to a horse sale. Mary told me this morning.'

'Mary told you? You mean you didn't know that Cade would be away for the day?' He gave her no chance to respond to the unjust accusation, his voice tinged with ice as he continued brusquely, 'Then I'm afraid that I shall have to ask you to bring them over. I need them immediately, and I can't afford the time to drive back for them.'

He gave her instructions on how to get to the building site, making her repeat them until he was satisfied that she had them correct. 'You'll find keys to the convertible in the top drawer of my desk. I'll see you in about an hour's time.' He paused, then added quietly. 'Just be careful, Stephanie.'

Warmth ran up her spine, and unconsciously her tone reflected it. 'I shall. Don't worry, Logan. I'll be fine.'

'I'm sure you will. I just don't want there to be any delay in getting those papers over here.'

Why, of all the self-centred, miserable... Adjectives flowed through her mind like water, but when she started to tell him what she thought she realised he'd hung up. She slammed the receiver down, half tempted not to take him his precious papers, but she had a good idea of how he might react!

It took longer than she'd anticipated getting to the construction site. First she had to run over to Mary's to tell her what had happened and collect Jessica. When Mary added her voice to the child's pleas to be allowed to stay and play with the twins, offering to look after Jessica for however long it took for Stephanie to get back, she accepted gratefully rather than drag the child out on such a miserable day. However that was just the first delay. Next she had to overcome her nervousness at driving the expensive Mercedes sports car. Logan drove a big black Lincoln Town car to and from work, using the small, sleek convertible only occasionally at night. Stephanie had never driven such a beautiful car before, but after a few miles gradually started to appreciate the power packed under the bonnet. It was just unfortunate that her enthusiasm made her fall foul of the local sheriff's department as she broke the strict fifty-five speed limit.

The officer was faultlessly courteous, but by the time he had checked out that she had permission to drive the car and sorted out her on-the-spot fine it was closer to two hours than one when she turned through the gates of the construction site. The rain was lashing down, a heavy grey sheet of water that made it difficult to see, and she slowed down to ease the car over the rough road. The work seemed to be in three phases, with several houses already built, some partially so, and another phase barely started.

Stephanie steered the car towards the site office she could see at the far side of the compound and slowed to a halt, breathing a sigh of relief that she'd finally made it. Hurriedly she gathered the file of papers from the passenger seat and opened the door, reeling back from the force of the rain that lashed into her face.

'Where the hell have you been? I've been waiting for those papers for almost two hours now.' Logan's hand was rough as he grasped her elbow and half lifted her from the car, his dark eyes glaring down at her, and Stephanie felt a totally understandable surge of anger. She'd driven sixty miles in the most foul weather, tangled with the law, and for what? To be greeted like this!

She wrenched her arm away and slammed the car door, uncaring that the rain was streaming over her head and shoulders, soaking her lightweight lemon sweatshirt. 'And it's lovely to see you too, Mr Ford! No, don't bother asking if I had any problems getting here. I *know* that was on the tip of your tongue, but to save you wasting your precious time the journey was fine, marvellous. There is nothing I like better than driving along strange roads on a day like this. In fact I enjoyed it so much that I stopped off for a little sightseeing along the way, got myself acquainted with how the local police department works. And I must say that officer was far more of a gentleman than you!'

He glowered back at her, bending slightly to stare straight into her face. 'Don't get smart, lady. I don't need one of your comedy routines right now.'

'No? I'd have said that was just what you needed. It might just manage to take the edge off your insufferable self-righteousness. What's it like, Logan, being so perfect? Don't you ever find it lonely on top of your ice mountain?'

For a moment she wondered if she'd pushed him just a shade too far. His whole body tensed, his big hands clenching around the heavy plastic folder, and a ripple of excitement ran through her at the idea that she seemed to have dented his composure. Then with a rough oath he swung away and disappeared inside the mobile office, letting the metal door clang shut behind him.

Stephanie blinked rapidly, feeling the tears stinging behind her lids. She couldn't even provoke him into an argument, that was how little he cared, and the thought cut like a knife in a wound that wouldn't heal. She turned back to the car then let her hand lie on the door-handle, knowing that she was in no fit state to drive right then. She had to get her emotions under control again before she set off.

Hunching her shoulders, she walked away from the office. She was so wet now that it made no difference if she got even wetter. She wandered aimlessly, finally coming to a halt on the bank of a small lake. She stared round, studying the layout of the site, realising without having any real knowledge of property in Florida that it would be a very exclusive area once it was completed. The houses were all built to overlook this lake, giving a feeling of space and openness not always found on small housing estates. Even the lake itself was being worked on, the banks dug back a few yards to deepen and widen it.

Slowly Stephanie turned in a circle, letting her gaze travel around the area as she tried to picture what it would look like when it was completed, and felt a sharp stab of pain at the sudden realisation that she wouldn't be here then. She'd be back in England with only her memories of this time and of Logan to hold on to.

Whether it was that thought that made her careless she had no idea. One minute she was standing on the edge of the bank, the next her feet were sliding from under her. She gave a sharp scream, then choked as muddy water filled her mouth. She struggled back to the surface and swam to the bank, clawing at the mud as she tried to lever herself out, but the rain had made the already loosened soil doubly unstable. The more she clawed at it, the more that came away, slithering down into her face. Breathlessly Stephanie leant against the muddy slope, forcing herself to calm down and think what she should do. The water came only to chest height, so it was unlikely that she would drown; she had to take things nice and calmly and find some way to get out.

It was all very well telling herself to stay calm, but quite another thing to do it when she discovered that even after a rest she just didn't have the strength to claw her way up the slippery bank. Although it was only about eight feet to the top, it was just too steep to get more than a few inches up it. After a dozen or more times of trying, she gave up, her whole body aching with strain, her legs trembling with the effort of holding her up. Although it was still quite warm, she felt chilled by the water she was standing in, her body temperature dropping second by second.

She dug her fingers into the mud and leant her head on her filthy arms, choking back the tears of fear. What was she going to do now? There was no point in shouting for help, because there was no one working on the site today because of the rain, and the office was too far away for Logan to hear her. It was hopeless.

She had no idea how long she lay there. Time seemed to have lost its meaning as exhaustion and cold took their toll. Several times she felt herself slipping down and she roused herself from the lethargy to claw her way back up the bank a few inches, but each time it happened it took more and more of her diminishing strength. She closed her eyes, letting her mind drift into blackness as she whispered Logan's name.

It was the anxiety in the voice shouting her name that roused her. Stephanie raised her head and stared round, taking a few seconds to understand where she was. Her whole body seemed to be numb, the cold seeping deep into her bones from lying partly submerged in the muddy water for so long.

'Stephanie! Answer me, woman!'

The sound was closer now, the harsh tones so achingly familiar that tears ran down her face. She forced a breath between her mud-caked lips and tried to shout back an answer, then screamed hoarsely as she felt herself slipping down into the water. Desperately she dug her fingers into the mud, feeling her nails tearing as she clutched at stones and roots to stop herself from going under the water again.

'Hold on. Don't try moving. Can you hear me, honey? Don't move!'

Her mouth tilted into a weak smile at the brusque instruction, knowing there was no way short of a miracle that she was going anywhere. She clung tightly to a rock embedded in the soil, hearing the rough sound of Logan's cursing as he slid down the bank and stopped beside her.

'All right, I've got you now. Do you think you can help if I try to push you up to the top?' He had his arm around the back of her waist, standing next to her in the muddy water. He looked so incongruous standing there like that, dressed to perfection in a pale grey suit that wouldn't be pale grey after this little adventure. Stephanie felt the most ridiculous urge to giggle and carry on giggling, but when she gave in to the urge there was a note of frenzy about the sound that shocked her.

'Stop that!' His hand caught her cheek a smart slap, cutting off the mounting hysteria. Stephanie stared at him with huge, shocked eyes, and saw his face tauten. Very gently he reached out and laid his knuckles against her cheek, his voice very soft. 'I had to do that, honey. This is no time to be getting hysterical. You can have all the hysterics you want once you're safely out of here. In fact I might join you.'

What an odd thing for him to say! She couldn't imagine him ever giving in to a hysterical outburst. However, before she really had time to dwell on it, he started pushing her up the bank. Stephanie tried to help, but she was so weak and cold after her partial submersion in the water that she had no strength left. It was down to Logan, and fortunately he had the strength for both of them.

With one last supreme effort he pushed her over the top, then rolled on to the muddy ground beside her, his chest heaving from the exertion. Stephanie took a shaky little breath, suddenly realising just how close she'd come to disaster. If Logan hadn't come looking for her...

'Don't.' He was closer than she'd realised, his brown eyes so dark that she could see tiny reflections of herself mirrored in them as he stared down into her frightened face. Slowly he brushed his thumb across her lips to wipe away the caked-on mud, then bent and kissed her hard and fiercely, almost as though he meant to punish her. Stephanie kissed him back, just as fiercely, knowing that now wasn't the time to pretend. Now, for these precious minutes, it was enough to lie there in the mud and feel Logan's mouth on hers making her feel so wonderfully alive.

He drew back slowly, his expression guarded, but he couldn't quite hide the glitter in those dark eyes as he studied her for one long moment then dragged himself to his feet. 'Come on. We have to get you out of those clothes. You're in danger of hypothermia.'

She forced a smile, feeling the hardening layer of mud on her face cracking as she moved her mouth. 'It doesn't feel that cold.'

'It has nothing to do with the weather in this case. Your body temperature has dropped with being stuck in that water for so long.' He bent and pressed his fingers to the mud-slicked skin at the base of her neck, concern crossing his face before he suddenly lifted her into his arms and started back from the lake. Stephanie lay against him, too weak to move or protest that she could manage. It felt so good to have him hold her like this for whatever reason he was doing it, too good to want him to stop.

He said nothing as he carried her, his long legs eating up the ground, his arms rock-steady as he held her as though she weighed next to nothing. Stephanie rested her head against the hard cushion of his shoulder, then realised that she was only spreading mud further over his suit. She drew back with a small murmur of regret and he glanced down at her, one brow lifting in silent query. He had mud streaked across his cheek and down the strong line of his jaw and should have looked ridiculous, but didn't. He looked tough and dependable and in control as usual, and the final barrier dropped from her mind. She loved him. It was as simple as that and just as complex. She loved him, but he would never thank her for telling him that.

Something of what she was feeling must have showed on her face, because he slowed abruptly. 'Are you all right?'

Stephanie took a slow breath, then let it whisper out from between her lips as she searched for an answer that wouldn't end up as a confession. 'You...your suit. It's ruined, and I'm making it worse by your carrying me.'

Anger seemed to explode from him. His hands tightened, his arms bruising as he drew her closer against his chest and glared down at her. 'To hell with the suit! You could have been stuck in that damned lake all night long if I hadn't found you, lady. Understand?'

It was a relief to get back on to familiar footings, to face his anger rather than her own emotions, which seemed to be rubbing her over-stretched nerves raw. 'I would have got out eventually...with or without your help!'

'Think so?' He deposited her abruptly on to her feet, then stepped back from her, watching dispassionately as she swayed unsteadily. When it looked as though she was going to crumple he suddenly picked her up again without a word and carried on walking, anger in every tense line of his body. Stephanie closed her mouth, accepting that it was pointless protesting when they both knew it was lies. She would never have got out of that lake without his help.

He stopped outside the completed show house, balancing her awkwardly as he felt in his pocket and found the key to unlock the door. Carrying her inside, he slammed it shut behind them with his foot, then marched towards the bathroom and set her down, seemingly uncaring that he'd just tracked mud across the expensive ivory and beige mix carpets. Stephanie knew better than to voice a protest, just stood silently gazing round the elegantly fitted room, then gasped when she felt him start to peel the sweatshirt off her.

'Stop that! What do you——?' The rest of her protest was muffled as he dragged the filthy cotton garment over her head before tossing it across the room and turning his attention to her once-white cotton trousers. His hands worked swiftly and adeptly on the zip, firmly pushing hers aside when she tried to stop him. Within minutes he had stripped her of all her clothes then calmly lifted her into the shower cubicle and turned on the water, adjusting it until it flowed smoothly over her shivering body. Stephanie stood dumbly under the cool spray as she closed her eyes and tried to pretend that it was the most normal thing in the world to have Logan undress her. But when he suddenly stepped in beside her and started to wipe the mud from her body, she started violently.

'No! Logan, really this isn't necessary. I can...' The words dried up as she pushed the wet hair from her eyes and suddenly realised that he too had shed his clothes, apart from dark boxer shorts which clung to his muscular flanks with the water. He was superbly built, his broad chest covered with a mat of dark gold hair, his waist lean and hard, his legs long and muscular. Stephanie stared at him helplessly for a moment before lifting her eyes to his face.

Something shone fleetingly in his eyes, an emotion so fierce that she almost reeled under the force of it. Then he seemed to make an almost superhuman effort to regain control as he reached towards her and ran his hands across her shoulders in broad, firm sweeps to wipe away the mud. 'We need to get that mud off you, then get you warm. It will be far easier and quicker if I help you, Stephanie. You don't need to feel embarrassed.'

She didn't, and that was what scared her half out of her mind. She had allowed no man this sort of liberty before nor ever wanted to. It was only Logan who made her ache to feel his touch. Only Logan whom she'd ever wanted in this way. Only Logan whom she would ever love.

She wasn't aware that she was crying silently until he slid his hand up and touched her cheek with a gentle finger. 'Don't, honey. You're quite safe now. Don't be afraid.'

His voice was achingly gentle and tender; it touched a chord inside her, making her cry all the harder, because he didn't understand, and, if he did, wouldn't care. She loved him! It should have been the most wonderful day of her life to realise it; instead it was the most painful, because it just made her realise how much she stood to lose when she left.

'Stephanie.' Her name was sweet on his lips, the sound of the rushing water beating on their two bodies muting it into a whisper that seemed to hold a note of yearning. She caught her breath, wishing she could believe what it seemed to promise, then felt herself go rigid with shock when she heard him say roughly, 'You scared the life out of me when I discovered the car and you not in it. I don't want to go through a time like that ever again!'

'Logan?' If she'd meant it as a question there was no time for an answer as he suddenly pulled her to him and kissed her almost as fiercely as before, his mouth relentless as he sought a response. There was a second, one tiny cold moment of sanity, when she knew she could be making the biggest mistake of her life, and then it was gone. She wanted him, wanted what he could make her feel. It might be all she would have to see her through so many long, lonely years.

She kissed him back with a passion which bordered on desperation, and felt the shudder that raced through his body flow into hers and chase away the lingering remnants of cold. When he started to deepen the kiss she opened her mouth eagerly, her hands sliding across the wet silk of his skin as she clung to his shoulders to keep her balance as her legs went weak. His arms wrapped even more tightly around her, drawing her to him so that her breasts brushed against his chest, the nipples hardening to tiny buds of desire as she felt the softly abrasive touch of his body hair. He groaned deeply, harshly, his hands urgent now as they smoothed over her skin, teasing, tormenting, arousing sensations she'd never dreamed of before.

Water sluiced over their entwined bodies, streamed over their faces, making their mouths slick as they kissed, their skin ultra-sensitive to each touch, each caress. When his hands slid up to cup her breasts she cried out, shaking with the force of her need as she felt the sweep of his tongue across each tight, wet nipple. Her fingers burrowed into his thick, wet hair, holding his head to her as she trembled with the magic he was creating.

When he suddenly started to draw back she clung, but he untwined her hands from around his neck and set her from him, his face carved into taut lines. 'This is where we stop, honey.'

Stephanie stared at him in confusion, her body still drugged with passion. 'Stop? But Logan——'

'I think I know what you're going to say, but it makes no difference.' He stepped from the shower and picked up a towel to rub his hair dry before glancing back at her. 'I didn't come prepared for this kind of encounter.'

'Prepared?' She couldn't seem to follow what he was saying, couldn't understand what was happening. One minute he was giving her a taste of heaven, then the next he was talking in riddles. She hugged her arms around her suddenly cold body, achingly conscious now of her nudity.

He sighed impatiently as he tossed her a towel. 'Yes. Look, I expect you're on the Pill or something and that the men in your life are more than happy with that arrangement, but I prefer to take care of that myself so that there can be no mistakes. Understand?'

He was so wrong that it would have been laughable if she didn't feel so much like crying. She dragged the towel around her, white-faced with pain. 'No, I'm not taking the Pill, Logan. I never have done.' She laughed bitterly. 'There's never been any reason to, because there have been no men in my life the way you mean. None!'

She regretted the words the moment she saw the shock on his face, but it was too late then. She stumbled from the shower and ran into the bedroom, closing the door behind her, but it was impossible to close her mind to what had happened. She'd been nearly mindless with desire just now, but Logan had been so unmoved that he'd coolly been able to call a halt. Perhaps she should thank him, because she'd never given a thought to the consequences of making love with him, but there was no way she could thank him for showing her just how little it had all meant to him.

CHAPTER NINE

THE rain had stopped and the sun was starting to break through the clouds. Stephanie drew the cream satin bedspread she'd taken from the bed tighter around her, but it did little to warm the chill from her bones. She had no idea how long she'd been standing there staring out of the window, but now the silence started to impinge on her consciousness. Where was Logan? Was he still in the house or had he left?

As though in answer to the question, the door suddenly opened and he came into the room. He tossed a yellow bundle on to the bed then walked over to the window, resting his arm against the frame as he stared out. A shaft of sunlight turned his red hair to fire, touched his skin with gold, and Stephanie felt her breath catch. He was wearing only his suit trousers, which clung wetly to his powerful legs, and nothing else, and she felt her senses stir before she deliberately looked away.

'Why, Stephanie? You must have had a reason, so tell me what it was, for heaven's sake!'

There was anger in his voice, and she shivered as she searched for an answer, not bothering to pretend that she didn't understand what he meant. What could she say to explain why she had been so willing...no, *eager*...to make love with him when she was a virgin? He wouldn't want to hear the real reason, the only reason that made sense to her—that she loved him!

'I wanted to. It's as simple as that, Logan.' Her voice was quiet, yet it seemed to set a flame to his temper. He slammed his fist against the wall, then turned to glare at her. 'Simple? Nothing you do is ever simple, lady. So don't give me that!'

'What else can I say? What would you like me to say?' She drew the satin bedspread tighter around her throat and stared back at him as steadily as she could. 'I couldn't remain a virgin all my life, could I? It had to happen some time.'

He swore softly, colourfully, his face tight as he caught her chin and lifted her face to glare into her eyes. 'But why now? Why with me?' When she tried to turn her head he held her, his eyes relentless as they bored into hers. 'No! Don't try making up excuses. I want the truth. If I hadn't stopped, then you and I would be in that bed even now making love, and I want to know why you chose me to bestow that honour upon.'

The tone of his voice stung, the icy sarcasm cutting deep, and she glared back at him just as angrily. 'Do you indeed? Well, maybe you should try explaining what you were up to. Why did *you* start it all in the first place, Logan? Especially if you knew you were going to end it just as quickly!'

Colour ran in a thin line along his cheekbones, and he let her go to swing back to stare out of the window. 'Don't get smart, honey. It doesn't suit you.'

'Why is it smart to want answers? Scared of admitting the truth yourself?'

'No.' His voice was like steel, hard and unyielding as it echoed around the room. 'The plain truth is that it was a natural reaction any man would have to finding himself in that sort of situation. We'd both had a shock, and emotions were running high even before I got you in that shower. After that, well...' He skimmed a deliberate look over her. 'You have a beautiful body, honey. Any man would want you if he held you naked in his arms. But it's why you were so responsive which disturbs me, especially in view of your claims to be so innocent. I don't allow anyone to take me for a fool, Stephanie.'

'I...I don't know what you mean.' It was hard to speak when it felt as though her life was lying in ruins. She'd thought those too brief moments in Logan's arms had been pure magic, something special, but now it seemed that he would have reacted the same way with any woman if the circumstances had been similar. It hadn't been *her* he'd been holding, kissing, driving almost insane with desire, and she didn't know how she was going to live with that knowledge.

'Then let me explain in simple terms. Using sex as a means to get what she wants seems to be a woman's main weapon. And how much more effective might that weapon be if the woman turns out to be a virgin? Even Amanda couldn't claim that advantage when she decided that I was just what she needed to relieve the boredom in her life.'

'You really imagine that I would have made love with you to get something from you?' She couldn't hide her shock, the cold horror she felt at the accusation. 'Tell me what, Logan. Tell me, damn you!'

He smiled coolly, unperturbed. 'I haven't worked that out yet, but I shall.'

'Then when you do, please tell me what it is!' She walked a few steps away from him then came back, too upset to stand still. 'You are so utterly wrong that it would be laughable if it weren't so insulting. I don't want anything from you. Not one single thing!' Apart from your love, her traitorous, empty heart added silently.

'Time will tell, Stephanie.'

'Time? I'm leaving in a week's time! There isn't enough time left to prove anything.'

'And maybe that's the key to it all.' He caught her by the shoulders, his fingers tightening against the slippery satin. 'I think I've been a little slow on the uptake, haven't I? Did you see this as the perfect way to persuade me to let you stay a while longer? Was that why you were so responsive...no, that isn't quite right...so *eager* to have me make love to you?' He laughed deeply, easing her closer as he ran his hand up her throat in a gesture that was more insult than caress. 'That's it, isn't it? Well, now that I have it all clear in my mind, then maybe I can be persuaded into extending your contract. It wouldn't be that much of a hardship, I'm sure.'

'No!' She caught his hand to stop him as it glided down towards her breast. The action made the cover slip a fraction, and she clutched it with her free hand, holding it desperately around her. 'You're wrong. I'm leaving soon. You know that was always the plan!'

'Do I?' He turned his hand to capture hers. 'Yet you were willing to make love with me without taking any precautions, if what you told me is correct. So what if there had been consequences of today's little interlude...a child, Stephanie? Or was that something you were planning on?'

'What? No!' She stared at him in horror, her face going pale. 'No, Logan. I...I never even thought about that.'

'No woman is that innocent today, not even one who claims to be a virgin.' He drew her closer, his hand sliding down over the curve of her hip. 'I must admit to feeling shocked when you told me that, but slowly it's all starting to make sense. You've already told me that you'll need to find a job when you get back to England, perhaps even need to find some place to live. Yet you have very little money left after your travels. Wouldn't it make sense to try to stay on here a while longer in the circumstances? I'm a rich man, Stephanie, as you very well know, and there is no denying that there is a certain spark of attraction between us. The thought of having me provide for you in exchange for a few... favours must have been attractive. And if there had been a child—one that was indisputably mine, of course—then that arrangement could have become permanent; isn't that right?'

'I... No! You're crazy, Logan. Completely crazy!' She pushed against him, making a grab for the bedspread as it suddenly started to slip to the floor, but with one hand still held firmly by him it was impossible to catch it.

'Crazy? No, I don't think so.' His eyes slid down her soft bare flesh, lingering on the swell of her breasts, and to Stephanie's shame she could feel the nipples start to harden in reaction to the slow waves of heat that built inside her. When Logan ran the palm of his hand down her from throat to thigh she shuddered helplessly and muttered a desperate protest. 'No! I don't want you to touch me, Logan.'

He laughed as he drew her closer so that her body brushed against his. 'Why lie, sweet? You like me touching you. And it's flattering to find that I can make you feel this way when you claim to be so innocent.' He traced the tip of a finger across one hard nipple, then looked straight into her shocked eyes. 'You can't pretend now, Stephanie. Not when your body is betraying how you feel so blatantly. You might have seen your chance before and decided to use your sexuality to your own advantage, but there's little to be gained now by denying that you want me. At least that's one point in your favour.'

'I didn't set out to do any such thing! You carried me into the house and started making love to me, Logan!' She had to convince him how wrong he was, but it was difficult to do that when he was touching her this way. She tried to ease away from him, but he held her firmly, his arm strong behind her waist.

'I don't recall having to use any degree of force.'

Her face flamed at the truth of what he said, but she stared back at him. 'No. But you've gone to all sorts of lengths to make it clear that you intended to keep our relationship on a business footing, so what made you suddenly change your mind?'

His eyes were hooded as they met hers. 'I already explained why. You're a beautiful and desirable woman and I wanted you. Despite your frequent accusations that I'm ice to the core, I'm just a normal man with all the normal urges.'

She didn't want to hear him repeating something which made her heart feel as though it were being slowly ripped into shreds. She pushed out of his arms, her voice filled with contempt. 'So normal that you're always in control, all the time? You had no difficulty in curbing those "urges" did you, Logan?' She laughed shrilly. 'I was right all along: you are made of ice!'

He stiffened at once, anger glinting in his eyes before he suddenly turned to stare out of the window. 'I'm not a fool, Stephanie. I learn by my mistakes.' He swung round suddenly, pinning her with a glance. 'If I'd followed my urges today and made love to you, then you could have become pregnant. Perhaps that was what you wanted, as I said.'

'No!' She dragged the bedcover around her, her whole body trembling. 'But if it had happened, then it would have been my responsibility, not yours!'

'Until you considered that the time was right to start making your claims on me.' His laughter was harsh and bitter as it filled the room. 'Just like Amanda! I never knew that she was expecting my child, you understand. She decided not to tell me, because by the time she found out her interest in me had waned. Amanda liked excitement, adventure, a man who would dance attendance on her. I disappointed her for all sorts of reasons, so that once she got over her initial fascination with me she went home to her parents and the wealthy lifestyle she was used to.

'It must have come as a shock to all of them when she found out she was carrying my child! But they had money and connections to see her through it without feeling any obligation to inform me that I had a daughter. I found out about Jessica almost by chance. It came as a shock, I can tell you, and I have no intention of ever repeating such a mistake. There will never be another child of mine born that I know nothing about, nor will I ever let any woman have that sort of a hold over me again!'

He strode from the room, leaving Stephanie with tears streaming down her face, but not for anything she had suffered. Perhaps those tears would come later, along with the regrets. For now all she could think of was the expression on Logan's face just now as he'd told her that bitter tale which explained so much. She only wished that he had trusted her enough to tell it to her sooner, but it was futile wishing for something that could never be.

Jessica was waiting at the window when they arrived at Mary's house to collect her. Logan had refused to let Stephanie drive the Mercedes, curtly informing her that it could stay where it was until the next day when one of his men could drive it back. He had driven them both home in the big black Lincoln in total silence.

Stephanie spent the journey staring out of the window, wishing there was something she could say to ease the tension, but there weren't any words to do that. Too much had gone on today for either of them to dismiss it lightly.

'I thought you were never coming back!' Jessica bounded out to meet them, then stopped dead, her eyes rounding in surprise. 'What's happened to your clothes, Stephie?' Jessica's face was a study as Stephanie climbed out of the car wearing the huge pair of yellow overalls that Logan had found for her. She had rolled the sleeves and legs up, but they still swamped her slender frame, and she knew she must look a fright. She forced a smile, determined not to let Jessica catch any hint of the tension between her and Logan.

'I managed to fall into the lake. Fortunately your father pulled me out, but my clothes were ruined. How do you like my new outfit?' She pirouetted for Jessica, holding the baggy folds of cloth away from her hips, and heard the child collapse into peals of laughter.

'I think I like your own clothes better! Honestly, Stephie, you do look funny, but so does Daddy! Look at his suit. It's a mess.'

Stephanie shot a quick glance at Logan, who had walked around the car, letting her eyes trace the lines of his powerful body in the mud-stained grey suit. He *should* have looked a mess all right if one considered the deplorable state of his clothing, but to her eyes he looked just as marvellous as ever. No matter what he wore he would always look like that to her, because she saw him with eyes filled with love, and that blinded her to any imperfections.

Her gaze lifted to tangle with his, and it suddenly felt as though the world faded into the background as the fiery memories surfaced with a speed which knocked her off balance: Logan bending to kiss her as she lay in the mud, his eyes glittering fiercely down into hers; Logan's hands sliding over her wet skin, setting off a chain reaction of sensations...

She had taken a half-step towards him, unaware of what she was doing, when a voice cut into her consciousness, abruptly bringing her back to her senses.

'And what's been going on here? Have I missed something?'

Stephanie shuddered as the sweet memories fell away to leave her cold and bereft once more. She turned to Cade, her smile unconsciously warmer than usual, fired by a kind of desperate desire to hang on to her sanity. 'You've not missed much. I fell into the lake at the construction site and, after rescuing me from a decidedly muddy fate, Logan found me this fetching little outfit to come home in.'

She performed another little twirl for Cade's benefit, keeping the brilliant smile fixed in place until her face felt as though it would crack from the effort it cost her.

'I see. And from the look of things, Logan didn't fare much better.' Cade's voice betrayed little, but Stephanie felt the colour steal up her cheeks in a guilty wash. She came to an abrupt halt, her eyes faintly beseeching as they met Cade's. He gave a faint, almost bitter smile, then moved towards Logan, stepping in front of Stephanie as he did so. 'This doesn't look like the best of times, but I could do with you coming over to the stables to run through the list of horses I bought today.'

'Give me ten minutes or so and I'll be with you.' Logan's voice was hard, his expression uncompromising as he walked past the other man and put Jessica into the car. He paused to glance back, his eyes running from Cade to Stephanie in a look which cut deep into her soul. 'I'll take Jess back. Don't take all day here. She'll need some of your attention, seeing as you've been gone so long.'

He was back to his autocratic self, issuing orders, expecting her to jump to attention. This afternoon and what had so nearly happened meant nothing to him.

'I'll just thank Mary, then I'll be there,' she muttered hoarsely. She turned away as Logan started the engine and pulled away, stumbling her way up the steps to the door of Mary's house.

'Careful.' Cade's hand was gentle but firm on her arm as he steadied her, and Stephanie shot him a thin little smile of thanks.

'His bark is worse than his bite, Stephanie. He doesn't mean half the things he says.'

'Doesn't he?' She gave a shrill little laugh. 'Oh, I disagree with that, Cade. I think he says exactly what he means, no matter whom he hurts!'

'And he's hurt you?' He shook his head, his fingers gentle as they moved to her chin and lifted her face. 'No. You don't need to answer that. I can see it in your face. You're in love with him, aren't you?'

There was a fleeting hint of regret in his green eyes before he let her go, looked away over the rolling pastures, and drew in a long, quiet breath.

Stephanie studied him in silence, not knowing what to say, how to reply to either the question or the situation. Was it just possible that Cade felt something for her? Something more than just friendship?

'Cade, I...' She stopped as he turned and smiled at her with an easy warmth, feeling the relief flooding through her that she'd been mistaken. She wouldn't want Cade to feel the sort of pain she was feeling.

'You do love that bad-tempered son of a gun, don't you?'

She laughed faintly. 'Yes. I think I do. Is it that obvious?'

He shrugged. 'To me, yes. To anyone else, I doubt it. So what do you intend to do about it, Stephanie? Are you going to tell him?'

'And have him laugh in my face? No, thank you! The one thing Logan doesn't want from me is any confession of undying devotion!'

'Are you sure of that? You aren't just reading what's on the surface and not looking deeper? Logan is a very complex person who hides his emotions from the world.'

'Well, if he feels anything for me then he's managed to hide it most successfully! Oh, don't get me wrong, Cade. He might feel a certain attraction to me, but that's all it is. There's nothing else.' She turned to stare towards the main house, then felt herself go cold when she spotted Logan standing on the porch watching them. Hurriedly she turned away, feeling the ready tears gathering behind her lids. What a day this had been! She'd fallen in love and had it thrown back in her face in the cruellest way possible.

'If that's the case then I can only suggest that you get away from here as soon as you can. Before you get hurt any more, Stephanie.'

Cade tipped his hat to her, then strode away, but it was several minutes before Stephanie knocked on Mary's door. She was due to leave in just over a week, but was Cade right to advise her to go before then? If she stayed, there was always the chance that Logan might guess how she felt about him, and she couldn't bear that, couldn't bear the cold amusement she would see on his face if he found that out. Yet once she left there would be no coming back. She would never see him again, and she didn't know if she could bear that either!

CHAPTER TEN

SHE had to leave.

For a whole night and most of the following day Stephanie had struggled with the decision, but as the time wore on she realised that Cade's advice had been right. It was tearing her apart being here and having Logan treat her as distantly as ever, as though nothing had happened between them at the construction site. It was better to make the cut quick rather than suffer this lingering agony.

She waited until Jessica was safely in bed before going to knock on the study door, her heart pounding as Logan bade her to enter. He wasn't sitting at the desk as she'd expected, but standing by the empty fireplace, one booted foot resting on the ornate brass fender. He'd barely spoken to her that day since he'd come back from work, and unconsciously she stiffened under the look he gave her. For a moment tension seemed to fill the air between them, then Logan straightened, one brow arching in question.

'Yes? Did you want to see me about something?'

His voice was cold and hard, cutting into her so swiftly that she came to a sudden halt halfway across the room. She clenched her hands as she willed the agony to abate to a level where she could think and remember what she'd spent so much time rehearsing, but all she could think of was the hardness in his deep voice, the lack of feeling. This man had roused her to a passion she'd never known existed yet now he spoke to her like a stranger, and she didn't think she could bear it!

'I asked what you wanted, Stephanie. I'm very busy, so I'd be grateful if you would tell me what it is.'

She flushed hotly, roused from her misery. She walked the rest of the way across the room, then stopped beside the desk and ran her fingers over the smooth polished wood before raising her head to look at him. 'I want you to make arrangements so that I can leave. Tomorrow if possible.'

'I see.' He moved to the desk and sat down behind it in the big brown leather chair, resting his forearms on its top as he stared down at his hands for a long moment before looking up at her. 'Why do you want to go so quickly? You must have a reason.'

'Of course I do! And you know very well what it is, Logan, so stop playing games.' There was a bitter note in her voice she couldn't help. 'After yesterday I'm sure you must be as anxious as I am to put an end to all this!'

'You seem to think you know me very well, Stephanie.' There was a hard edge to his voice now, and she glanced warily at him, but it was impossible to tell what was causing it. With a tiny ragged sigh she pushed the unease aside and carried on.

'I don't claim to know anything apart from the fact that you probably can't wait to be rid of me.'

'And what if I was to tell you that you are mistaken, that in fact I would like you to stay on here... on a more permanent basis? What would you say to that?' He leant back in the chair so that it creaked as it took his formidable weight. In the glow from the desk lamp his face was all stark angles and deep grooves, his eyes so dark that they appeared black. Stephanie searched his face, her breath catching so tightly that she felt almost dizzy as she tried to understand what he meant. Why did he want her to stay, and what did he mean about a permanent basis?

'I...' Her throat was thick, the words trapped there by the tension so that she had to fight to free them. 'I don't understand, Logan. Why would you want me to stay when you've always made it plain that's the last thing you would want?'

He ran a hand over his hair in a gesture which might have seemed nervous in anyone else, but Logan wasn't a man who suffered from nerves. He was always in control, as she knew only too clearly. The thought made her repeat the question far more sharply, and she started as he suddenly pushed back the chair and got up. He came around the desk then stopped, standing far too close to her for her peace of mind. She could smell the clean scent of his body, almost feel the heat which radiated from his skin, and her heart leapt in helpless response.

'I think we have both made our feelings very plain, especially yesterday.' He took her words and turned them back on her, smiling when he saw her turn her head away so that he couldn't see the expression in her eyes. He turned it back, studying the uncertainty and embarrassment which barely hid the hunger she felt at his touch.

He held her there for a long moment, as though searching for an answer to a question he hadn't asked, then suddenly let her go and walked over to the window that overlooked the paddock at the rear of the house. Night was falling, darkening the rolling countryside, stealing the colour from the emerald grass and azure sky, but the view still held a beauty which could draw the soul. She loved this place, loved the space, the feeling of freedom, and she was going to miss it when she left. Her eyes moved to Logan, following the lines of his tall, powerful body, and inside she felt the tears starting to fall. She was going to miss Logan even more!

It was that more than anything that made her ask the same question once again but in a much different tone. If there was a chance that he wanted her to stay because he cared for her, then she would never throw it away.

'Why do you want me to stay?'

He turned from the window, his face quite blank. 'For many reasons, not least of which is the fact Jessica is so fond of you.'

Her heart ached at the reply, but she stood firm, praying that if she stood there long enough she would hear the reply she wanted to hear so much. 'I am very fond of her too, but you've always known that. So why should it suddenly make a difference to your plans?'

'Because I've had time to re-think and see possible flaws in those plans.' He shrugged lightly. 'I had just assumed that I would find a suitable housekeeper-cum-nanny for Jessica and that would be that. However, I've come to realise that she needs more than that. She needs someone she can really love and grow close to, a permanent addition to her life, and hired help isn't the answer. What happens if I do find someone suitable and then she leaves for whatever reason? Where does that leave Jess?' He moved from the window and walked towards Stephanie, stopping just a few feet away. 'She's been through enough, and I won't put her through any more upset. That's why I want you to agree to stay on here, Stephanie, but in a different role than the one you've played so far.'

'Different? How? I don't understand.' Her voice grated shrilly through the heavy silence, and he smiled as though he understood the reason for it.

'I want you to marry me and stay on as my wife. It's as simple as that.'

'Marry you?' She had to grasp hold of the desk as her legs threatened to give way. She must have misheard!

'Yes. It's a perfect solution to all our problems. And after yesterday I don't think that it will be any hardship for either of us.' He ran a lazy finger across her parted lips, hearing the soft gasp of her breath with just the flicker of a smile. 'We're obviously sexually compatible, so I can't see any reason why our marriage shouldn't be a fair success, can you? It would be the perfect solution for all of us, and, most importantly, for Jessica.'

The perfect solution. Did he really imagine it was that? She backed away from him, her body trembling as she held on to her control. 'No! It's the most ridiculous thing I've ever heard!'

'Why?' He followed her, closing the distance between them as he backed her up against the edge of the desk. 'You've admitted that you're fond of Jessica, and you seem to enjoy being here on the farm. And you and I do seem to be capable of striking sparks off one another... remember?' He caught her by the shoulders and drew her to him as he smiled into her shocked eyes. 'Or perhaps you need something to jog your memory.'

'No! Logan, I——' His mouth stopped her protests, his lips warmly persuasive as they covered hers and sought a response. Stephanie held herself rigid, fighting the traitorous feelings of desire his touch brought instantly to life. All last night she had dreamt of this, of having Logan holding her and kissing her, and now it seemed those dreams had come true.

Desire spiralled in a dizzyingly hot surge, and she moaned as she put her hands on his shoulders to push him away, but then his tongue slid between her lips to deepen the kiss and she found her hands lingering on the hard muscles, her fingers tightening to hold him.

His arms tightened around her, drawing her closer to his body so that she could feel the hard pressure of his arousal against her, sending answering ripples of passion spinning through her. When he caught her hips and moved her slowly against him she shuddered, having to cling to him to stay upright.

He drew back slowly to look into her passion-filled eyes and smiled with undisguised triumph. 'It isn't a lie, is it, my sweet? We light fires inside one another all right.'

'But it isn't enough, Logan. You must see that!' She wedged her arms between them to try to ease herself away from the disturbing contact with his body, but his hands remained on her hips, holding her locked against the powerful length of his thighs.

'I can see no such thing. What do you want, Stephanie? Story-book declarations of undying love?' He laughed harshly, his bitter-chocolate eyes mocking. 'Love is the biggest fallacy of all time. Something thought up by dreamers who need to believe there's something out there to fill their lives! This is what's real, Stephanie.' He pulled her into sharp contact with his aroused body, making his meaning more than clear, and something inside her died in that instant.

'Let me go, Logan.' There was no emotion in her voice now, no anger, no pain, no passion. She felt empty and drained, as though someone had stolen her ability to feel those things. Something about her tone must have got through to him, because he let her go and stepped back, watching with a shuttered expression as she ran shaking hands over her skirt to smooth the fine soft cotton before she continued just as quietly, 'Yesterday you virtually accused me of planning what you've just suggested, and it was as ridiculous then as it is today. I can't accept your offer, I'm afraid. I shall just be grateful if you would book me a seat on a plane home as soon as possible.'

She turned to walk to the door, her legs trembling so that each step seemed like a hundred. She was almost there when he spoke, anger shimmering across the room towards her. 'You will regret this, Stephanie. It was a damned good offer and I shan't repeat it!'

She glanced back at him for just a moment, then opened the door and left without saying a word, because there was nothing she could say. He was right: she would regret it. She would regret it time and again in all the long years to come and wonder why she hadn't accepted rather than live her life without him. But she knew that to accept was to commit herself to more heartache than she could handle. To marry Logan when he cared nothing for her would be the worst thing she could ever do. Sex would never be a substitute for love.

'Come on, Stephie! Hurry up. Cade says that I can feed the foal this morning.'

Jessica called out to hurry her along, and Stephanie did her best to shake off the cold mantle of misery, but it was impossible. All night long she'd lain awake thinking about Logan's offer, calling herself every kind of a fool for refusing it. In her heart she knew she'd done the right thing, but that didn't help. The temptation to tell him that she had changed her mind had been so strong that she'd almost succumbed to it over breakfast, but had somehow managed to control the urge. He had curtly informed her that he had managed to book her on a flight in five days' time, and now all she could think of was how she would get through the coming days without begging him to let her accept the offer to stay. It would be the biggest mistake of her life to do that, yet she wasn't confident that she could resist making it when she loved him so much.

'How are you, Stephanie? You look very uptight about something this morning.' Cade's deep voice broke into her musings, and she forced a smile for him, realising they'd arrived at the stables without her being aware of it.

'I'm fine. Just a bit distracted, that's all.'

'Sure?' He bent to peer into her face, his green eyes darkening when he saw the shadows under her eyes and the lines of strain which tugged the corners of her mouth down. 'Is it Logan?'

There was such quiet sympathy in his tone that the ready tears started to her eyes and she turned away, focusing on the stable block, where she could see Jessica hanging over one of the half-open doors, stroking Dream Dancer's nose. 'Who else? I wish I knew what to do, Cade.'

He touched her arm gently. 'You know I'll help any way I can.'

She gave him a broken little smile, wiping her knuckles across her damp eyes. 'I know. Thank you. I just wish I could get away from here...now!'

'I thought the last thing you wanted was to leave?' There was a faint echo of something in the question, but Stephanie was too caught up in her own misery to hear it.

'I think it was until last night.' She laughed shakily. 'Logan asked me to marry him. Did you know that?'

'No. And what did you tell him?'

'What do you think? Ironic, isn't it? The right question that he asked me, but for all the wrong reasons!' The tears slid down her cheeks now unheeded as she stared up at the dark-haired man with everything she felt for Logan in her eyes. 'I love him so much, yet he didn't want to marry me because he felt the same way. Oh, no. Mr Ice-Cold Ford doesn't feel those sort of emotions. Love is beneath him! He wanted to marry me because he felt it would be good for Jessica to know that I would be a permanent part of her life! The fact that he and I aren't totally indifferent to one another was an added bonus, of course.'

'I see. So when are you leaving?'

'Not until next Monday. That's the earliest he could get me on a flight.'

'But you would prefer to leave sooner than that? Is that it?'

Stephanie fumbled in her pocket for a handkerchief, then accepted the one Cade silently handed to her. 'Yes. I'm so afraid that if I stay I'll agree, and that would be a mistake, Cade. A huge mistake!'

'Are you sure?' He stared past her, his face blank as he looked across the fields. 'Isn't there a chance that you can make Logan fall in love with you, given enough time?'

She shook her head sadly. 'I don't believe that you can *make* another person love you. If it's not there... well...'

Cade was silent for a long while, his darkly handsome face set. Stephanie looked at him curiously, suddenly strangely uncomfortable. Was she missing something here, letting her own misery cloud her mind? But just as she was starting to worry what she could say he looked at her and smiled. 'I guess you're right. Love can't be forced. However, there is something I can do for you, Stephanie. I can get you on to an earlier flight.'

'You can? But Logan said that they were all booked up.'

'I have connections, shall I say. Do you want me to try?'

She took a long sobering breath, then nodded quickly. 'Yes. I want to leave here as soon as possible, Cade. I... I don't think I can take any more of this.'

He patted her arm, then turned to walk across to the office. 'Leave it with me, Stephanie. I'll see what I can do.'

'I don't know how to thank you, Cade. You've been so kind.'

He stopped in mid-stride, his face shadowed by the brim of his hat as he looked over his shoulder at her. 'Just promise me that you'll be happy, Stephanie. That's all I ask. I don't want to think of you spending the rest of your life pining for Logan.'

She forced a wobbly grin. 'I don't want to think about that either, but I don't think I shall ever really get over him. He's the most infuriating, impossible man, but I love him, Cade. So help me, I do love him!'

'Then he's a bigger fool than I imagined if he lets you go!' He strode into the office and slammed the door with unaccustomed violence, leaving Stephanie alone with her thoughts.

'Logan,' she whispered brokenly. 'Logan!'

The sound echoed into the distance and disappeared on the wind.

Everything was packed. Stephanie carried her case out to the porch and set it down. From the direction of the stables came the sound of an engine, but she didn't look round until the car drew up at the bottom of the steps and Cade climbed out.

'Is this everything?' he asked quietly as he climbed the steps and picked up the case to carry it to the waiting vehicle. Stephanie nodded, unable to speak as pain swamped her. She stared across the fields through a veil of tears, trying her hardest to memorise the view to take with her. She would never forget this place, or Jessica, or...

Her mind closed on the name, unable to bear the thought of never seeing Logan again. She took a shaky breath, then walked down the steps and slid into the passenger seat, forcing a smile for Cade, who was watching her with concern shadowing his eyes.

'It isn't too late to change your mind, Stephanie.' He held the door open as he bent to look directly into her strained face. 'You can always accept Logan's offer and stay.'

'No, I can't. It would be the worst thing I could ever do. I love him, but I can't live with him inside a loveless marriage, as he wants. It would tear me apart.'

'And what do you think leaving like this is doing?' He closed the door, then hesitated, a strange indecisiveness on his face before he seemed to come to a sudden decision. 'I just need to make a phone call before we go. I won't be long.'

He disappeared inside the house, and Stephanie rested her head back against the seat and closed her eyes as she prayed for enough strength to get through the next few hours. When Cade had offered to get her a seat on a plane she'd never imagined that he would manage it so quickly. She'd barely had time to pack her things after he'd come back and curtly informed her there was one available on the afternoon flight. Jessica had been heartbroken when Stephanie had explained to her that she was leaving, but there had been no way she could just go without telling the child first. It had hurt to see Jessica's tears and hold the small body close and feel it shaking with sobs, but the past few weeks had done a lot to help Jessica cope with the coming parting. The child had gained a certain resilience she'd not had before which would see her through this upset. She would survive, but would Stephanie? That was more to the point.

'Right, we may as well be on our way, then.' Cade slid behind the wheel and started the car, shooting her a level look before pulling away from the house. 'Sure this is what you want, now?'

Stephanie shook her head, a wryly tremulous smile touching her mouth. 'No, it isn't what I want, but it's what I know I have to do.'

'Fair enough.' He deliberately changed the subject, keeping the conversation to impersonal topics as he drove towards the airport. He parked in one of the huge airport car parks, then went into the airport with Stephanie. She was glad of his help, because she felt as though everything were happening at a distance, as though none of it was real. It was only when she noticed him glancing at his watch for the third time in as many minutes that she realised she was probably playing on his kindness.

She forced a smile, her blue eyes filled with genuine warmth as she looked at him. 'I'm sorry, Cade. I must be keeping you from all sorts of jobs you would rather be doing than nursemaiding me.'

'Not at all. There's nothing so urgent that it can't wait.' His voice was smoothly courteous and friendly, but there was a certain tension about the look he skimmed round the busy terminal that belied the words.

'You're just being kind. I shall be all right by myself, honestly. You go on back to the farm.' She held her hand out, blinking back the tears at the thought of the impending parting. 'I don't know how to thank you, Cade, for all your kindness and everything you've done for me. And I don't just mean today getting me this seat on the plane. You've helped me throughout the time I've been here, and I won't ever forget you.'

'And I won't ever forget you, Stephanie.' Ignoring her outstretched hand, he caught her by the shoulders and bent to kiss her lightly on the cheek. 'You're a very special woman, Stephanie. I only wish that I'd——'

'Get your hands off her, Rylance!'

There was no mistaking that voice, no mistaking the anger which echoed in it, turning the harsh tones to pure steel. Stephanie jumped as though she'd been hit, her head swinging round to pinpoint Logan standing just behind her, every line of his powerful body radiating menace.

'Logan!' His name whispered from her lips, but he seemed not to hear her, his whole attention focused on the dark-haired man who was still holding her by the shoulders.

'I said get your hands off her! That was surely plain enough for you to understand, wasn't it, Rylance?'

Cade smiled tightly, his hands remaining exactly where they were on Stephanie's shoulders. 'Oh, I understand all right, but do you, Logan?'

Logan's brows lowered, his face settling into lines that made Stephanie's heart turn over in sudden fear, although she couldn't understand what was happening. When he took a deliberate step towards her and Cade, his big hands clenching into fists, she stepped in front of him and glared into his face.

'Stop that! I don't know what you think you're doing, Logan Ford, but——'

He picked her up and set her to one side, abruptly stopping her protests as he closed the distance between him and Cade. 'You saw this as your chance, didn't you, Rylance? You've been wanting Stephanie from the first moment you met her!'

Stephanie went still with shock as she stared from one set face to the other, but the two men seemed unaware of her presence as they faced each other.

'And why should it matter to you, Logan? What if I do want Stephanie? You don't want her, do you? So why be such a dog in the manger about it?'

The words were barely out before Logan's fist hit him hard on the jaw. He staggered back under the impact of the blow, but didn't fall. Straightening up, he ran a hand over the reddening swelling forming on his jawbone, his green eyes glittering as he stared back at the other man.

'I'll let you get away with that once, Ford, but don't make the mistake of trying it again.' His eyes skimmed to Stephanie's horrified face before cutting back to the red-haired man with a faintly mocking smile. 'What's it like, Logan, suddenly realising that you're human after all? A sobering experience, I imagine, but just be glad that you realised what you were about to lose before it was too late.'

He swung round on his heel and strode away without another word, leaving Stephanie staring after him for a long dumb second before abruptly realising what was going on. She started after him, calling his name, but stopped when a hard hand closed over her arm.

'Leave him be.'

She turned on Logan, pain and fear sending her temper spiralling. 'Just who do you think you are, ordering me about? I no longer work for you, Logan Ford, and if I want to go after Cade to see that he's all right then I shall!'

'Over my dead body! I've been far too tolerant about you and him already.'

'Tolerant? About me and Cade?' Hands on hips, she faced him squarely, her blue eyes filled with fire, her dark hair wisping around her flushed face. 'Who the hell said that you could sit in judgement on our friendship? What right do you have to be "tolerant" of anything I do?'

Her anger set light to his. He dragged her to him, glaring down into her face. 'I have every damned right in the world!'

'Oh, yes? Why? Just answer me that, Mr Perfect. Why?' She refused to back down, despite the tremors which were coursing through her. She was about to leave, and the last thing she wanted was to leave with the memory of this bitter scene for company.

'Because I love you! That gives me all the rights in the world.'

Said in that hard, unbending tone, it took a few blank seconds for the meaning of the words to sink in to her brain. When it did she stared at him in open-mouthed shock and saw his face soften.

'I love you, Stephanie. That's why I couldn't bear to see Cade holding you before, why I can't bear the thought of you and him having a close friendship. I'm jealous, so help me!'

There was a wry ring to his tone now, and she shook her head. She wanted to believe what he was telling her so much that it hurt, but how could she when only last night he had told her that he didn't believe in love? She wrenched herself away from him and turned and ran, pushing her way through the crowds, her only thought to escape whatever torment he'd dreamed up to hurt her with this time.

'Stephanie!' His voice was gentle now as he called her name, the deep tones echoing with a tenderness that slowed her frantic footsteps. She glanced over her shoulder, watching warily as Logan came to a halt a few yards behind her. He ran a hand over his hair, and she was shocked to see that it was shaking. He took one slow step closer, watching her all the time, as though he was afraid she'd run again.

'I know it's expecting a lot to ask you to believe me, but it's the truth, honey. I do love you with all my heart, my soul and parts of me I never knew existed before. If you feel anything at all for me, then won't you give me just a little time to try and convince you?'

He held his hand out to her, palm upwards. Stephanie stared at it, every bit of her consumed with tension and fear. She looked up into his face, searching for something, some sign that would make her take that one huge step towards him, that one precious step towards belief that he was telling her the truth, and found it in the tormented darkness of his eyes.

'Logan!' His name was a celebration of joy as it tore from her lips. It seemed to break the constraint he'd imposed upon himself, because he strode towards her and swept her into his arms, holding her so close as he kissed her with a fiery hunger that she could hardly breathe. When he raised his head she smiled at him through her tears, touching a finger to his mouth in a loving, betraying caress that made him shudder.

'I love you, Logan,' she whispered softly. 'I love you so much.'

A spasm ran through him and he hugged her close, holding her against his heart with a tenderness that defied description before suddenly loosening his hold and staring round the bustling airport with a self-mocking grimace. 'Let's get out of here, shall we? What we need is a little privacy, and Orlando airport isn't the place for it.'

Stephanie smiled as she suddenly noticed all the interest they were attracting, unashamed by it. She loved Logan, and as far as she was concerned the whole wide world could know!

Logan took her hand and led her to the car park, putting her into his car before getting in and taking her in his arms. The kiss was everything she could have dreamed of, leaving her weak and shaking when it finally ended. Logan smiled with a touch of his old arrogance when he saw her expression, curving her close against his side as he brushed a fleeting kiss across her swollen lips then drew back before she could respond. 'We need to talk, my sweet. I know this isn't the most romantic of settings, but we need to do so without any interruptions. If we go straight back to the farm, then Jessica will be there wanting to know what's happened and if I've kept my promise to make you come back.'

'Was it Jessica who told you that I had gone?' She snuggled against him, loving the feel of his body so close to hers.

'No. We have Cade to thank for that.' He smiled, albeit a trifle grimly, when he felt her start of surprise. 'He phoned my office and left a message to say that you were leaving on the afternoon flight.'

'He did?' She stared at him in surprise, then suddenly remembered the phone call Cade had needed to make. So that was where he'd been ringing!

'Mmm. Damned lucky that I happened to phone through to check if there were any messages. I'd been at the site, and it was just by chance that I did so, otherwise you would have left and I wouldn't have known anything about it until I got back home tonight!' He kissed her hard and hungrily, as though the very thought disturbed him. Stephanie felt her heart swelling with joy. She clung to him, murmuring a soft protest when he determinedly set her a little away from him.

'This needs sorting out, my love. I want a future with you, and I want it based on the truth.'

She nodded, knowing he was right, then asked a question asked by lovers since the beginning of time. 'When did you know that you were in love with me?

Last night you seemed to mock the whole idea, yet today...'

He grinned, then suddenly laughed out loud. 'Last night I was fighting tooth and nail against my feelings. I wouldn't admit how I felt even to myself, but today when I suddenly realised that I was going to lose you if I didn't do something... Well, it's amazing how that can concentrate a man's mind!'

'Today? Then thank heavens that Cade did call you. I shall always be grateful to him for that!'

'Not too grateful, I hope.' There was only partial mockery in the growling tone of Logan's voice, making her realise that he was still unsure of her feelings for his manager. She brushed his jaw with a lingering kiss, then curled her fingers between his long ones and lifted his hand to her lips. 'Cade and I were only ever friends. He knew how I felt about you ages ago, almost before I knew it myself.'

Logan seemed to make a determined effort to relax. 'Cade and I go back a long way. He knows me better than anyone else, I imagine.'

'He... he told me that he'd met Amanda, but he wouldn't tell me anything about her.'

There was a question in her voice, and Logan sighed softly. 'Amanda was a mistake. I enjoyed her company when we first met, but I was never in love with her.'

'Where did you meet?'

'At her parents' house in Palm Beach. I was just setting up my company then, and her father hired me to renovate the house they had there, a huge place. Amanda's parents were as rich as could be, the top drawer of Palm Beach society. They didn't take kindly to their daughter displaying an interest in a man who was basically a construction worker from the wrong side of Daytona.' He laughed softly, but without any bitterness. 'And I did come from the wrong side of town, the wrong background, everything. My parents were just about as poor as hers were rich. My mother walked out when I was fifteen, and after that my father spent his time in an alcoholic stupor until he died a couple of years later.

'I drifted around a bit until I got into construction work by accident and found I had a certain flair for it. I worked every hour I could to get some money behind me, and was just starting to make a go of things when I took the job at Amanda's parents' house. She made her interest in me known almost immediately, following me around, flirting. I think I was something different in her life, a new experience.'

'So you two decided to live together?' She couldn't quite hide the pain she felt at the thought of the life Logan had shared with the other woman. He swore softly, tilting her face so that he could kiss her gently.

'It wasn't any decision of mine. I finished the job there, then one day out of the blue Amanda turned up on my doorstep with her suitcase. She'd decided to move in with me, and I let her.' He shrugged. 'I'm not proud of the fact, but that's how it was. I'd never felt much for any woman. I think the way my mother just upped and left made me wary of giving anyone that much of a hold over me. I certainly didn't love Amanda, but she was beautiful and fun to be with, so I took what she so willingly offered. Then understandably she got tired of living with a man who was up at five and worked until eight. She wanted more excitement and less boredom, I imagine. She packed up and left, and I wasn't sorry to see her go, if you want the truth.'

'But there was Jessica,' she reminded him softly. 'And I know how much you love her. She must have been something good from the relationship.'

Pain flashed across his face, and he leant his head back and closed his eyes. 'Yes, there was Jessica...when I eventually found out about her. I think I told you that I knew nothing about her at first. It was only when Amanda had a few too many drinks one night and was feeling bored with the current man in her life that I found out. She phoned me up, possibly to see if we could get back together, I don't know. She let slip about Jess then. Oh, she tried to deny it later, as did her parents, but it was farcical really. There I was in their sitting-room, listening to this pack of lies about her not being my child, and in she ran.' He smoothed a hand over his thick hair. 'It's about the only time I've given thanks for this. One look at that child and there was all the proof I needed!

'Amanda caved in and admitted it after that, although I had to put a certain amount of pressure on her parents.' His tone was grim, and Stephanie held back a shudder, knowing only too well what a strong adversary Logan could be.

'So they agreed to let you see Jessica?' she queried gently.

'In the end, yes. I was in a stronger financial position by then and could hold my own against them. I was determined that I would have a say in my child's future, and made Amanda sign papers to that effect. Thank heavens that I did, because I would have had trouble getting custody of Jess when Amanda died otherwise. As it was, I had to threaten her mother that I would go to the papers with the fact that Amanda had been drinking when she was killed. I didn't want my daughter brought up in the same way that Amanda had been, spoilt by money and power.'

'Is that why you won't allow Jessica to see her grandmother? She misses her, Logan. She should be allowed to keep up the family contact.'

'I know. Maybe it's something we can sort out between us after we're married.' He turned to her, suddenly serious, a faint uncertainty on his face which touched her deeply by being so out of character. 'You will marry me, won't you, Stephanie? I don't think I could bear to let you go now.'

She smiled, drawing out the moment to savour the sweetness of it better. 'If you're sure that you want me, and sure that it isn't just to get a permanent companion for Jessica.'

'Jessica doesn't enter into this for once!' He pulled her into his arms, his face almost fierce. 'I love you, I want you, and I won't allow you to leave me! Understand?'

'Completely.' She kissed him on the mouth, nipping his lower lip and loving the faint groan he gave at the deliberately seductive caress. 'It seems that I don't have a lot of choice, do I?'

'None at all. You either agree now or I carry you off somewhere and spend the next few days convincing you that you can't live without me.'

'Now that does sound tempting!' She gasped when he punished her teasing with a searing kiss which left her breathless. When she could speak again she smiled into his eyes, letting him see all the love she felt for him. 'Yes, I'll marry you, Logan. I can't think of anything I want more in the whole world than to be your wife.'

He kissed her again with aching tenderness. 'Thank you, Stephanie. I've never asked any woman to marry me before—never wanted to, in fact. I guess I formed a low opinion of marriage from early on. My parents' marriage was never a happy one; they spent more time arguing than anything else, mainly over the fact that my father couldn't give Mother the life she wanted. It coloured my view and made me determined to steer clear of any sort of commitment. Not that it was difficult, mind you. None of the relationships I had made me want to change my mind; if anything they just proved that I was right.'

'Not even the relationship with Amanda?'

'*Especially* not with Amanda. Amanda's main concern was Amanda. There was never any doubt about that. That spell with her reinforced everything I'd believed in. And I saw no need to change my views until you came along and slowly and insistently started to worm your way into my heart.'

'Mmm, all sounds very convincing, apart from the small matter of the lovely Melissa Cooper. You seemed to take a real interest in her, when you consider the amount of time you spent with her.' Jealous sparks flashed in her eyes, and he laughed deeply.

'I spent one evening with Melissa and was bored rigid, if you want the truth. That's the reason why I came home so early, and was I glad that I did when I found you there, looking like the embodiment of every man's dreams!'

She smiled at the compliment. 'I thought your only dream was the American one—you know, making a lot of money, having a wonderful lifestyle.'

'It used to be until I met you. Now you are what fills my dreams. You are what I want from life. You, me and Jessica; that's enough for any man to build his dreams upon.'

Tears glimmered in her eyes at the tender assertion. 'Oh, Logan, I do love you.'

'I hope you do, because I shall never let you go now.' He kissed her hard, then let her go to start the car. 'I just hope you aren't planning on making me wait too long before I put that ring on your finger. I doubt if I'll have the sort of will-power again I had the other day at the site, but when I make love to you I want it to be perfect... for you to be my wife.'

Stephanie flushed softly at the note of intimacy in his voice. 'I thought you didn't really care then, that I was just another female body.'

He swore softly. 'I cared too damned much! That's the main reason I knew I had to call a halt. Some sixth sense told me that if I once made love to you then that would be it, I would be under your spell for life, and I wasn't ready for that then. I was still running scared and afraid to face up to my feelings. So will you marry me as soon as I can make all the arrangements, and put me out of my misery?'

'I'll marry you tomorrow if it's possible, Logan.'

He smiled when he heard her soft reply. 'That's what I hoped you'd say, but what about your friends and family?'

She shook her head. 'There's really only Rachel and Laura, and they'll understand if we have the wedding first and then invite them over later.'

'The two friends you went on holiday with?' His hands tightened on the wheel, his voice deliberately expressionless. 'Am I being selfish in wanting to keep you here, Stephanie? You might have planned on seeing more of the world before you settled down.'

She leant over and kissed him quickly, understanding the fleeting uncertainty. 'I'm not like Amanda. I've found what I want, Logan. All my dreams have come true. Everything I want is here because *you* are here and you are all I shall ever need to make me happy.'

He captured her hand and pressed it to his lips, his eyes loving her. 'Then there's nothing more to say, apart from let's go home and tell Jessica the wonderful news.'

Her fingers tightened around his, her face filled with love as she smiled back at him. 'Yes, let's go home.'

Full of Eastern Passion...

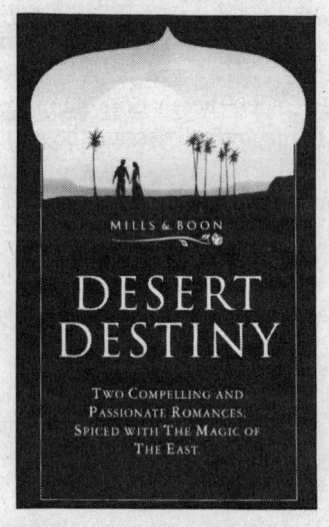

MILLS & BOON

DESERT DESTINY

TWO COMPELLING AND
PASSIONATE ROMANCES,
SPICED WITH THE MAGIC OF
THE EAST.

Savour the romance of the East this summer with
our two full-length compelling Romances,
wrapped together in one exciting volume.

AVAILABLE FROM 29 JULY 1994   PRICED £3.99

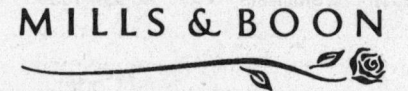

MILLS & BOON

*Available from WH Smith, John Menzies, Volume One, Forbuoys, Martins,
Woolworths, Tesco, Asda, Safeway and other paperback stockists.
Also available from Mills & Boon Reader Service, FREEPOST,
PO Box 236, Croydon, Surrey CR9 9EL. (UK Postage & Packing free)*

Next Month's Romances

Each month you can choose from a wide variety of romance with Mills & Boon. Below are the new titles to look out for next month, why not ask either Mills & Boon Reader Service or your Newsagent to reserve you a copy of the titles you want to buy – just tick the titles you would like and either post to Reader Service or take it to any Newsagent and ask them to order your books.

Please save me the following titles:	Please tick	✓
THE SULTAN'S FAVOURITE	Helen Brooks	
INFAMOUS BARGAIN	Daphne Clair	
A TRUSTING HEART	Helena Dawson	
MISSISSIPPI MOONLIGHT	Angela Devine	
TIGER EYES	Robyn Donald	
COVER STORY	Jane Donnelly	
LEAP OF FAITH	Rachel Elliot	
EVIDENCE OF SIN	Catherine George	
THE DAMARIS WOMAN	Grace Green	
LORD OF THE MANOR	Stephanie Howard	
INHERITANCE	Shirley Kemp	
PASSION'S PREY	Rebecca King	
DYING FOR YOU	Charlotte Lamb	
NORAH	Debbie Macomber	
PASSION BECOMES YOU	Michelle Reid	
SHADOW PLAY	Sally Wentworth	

If you would like to order these books in addition to your regular subscription from Mills & Boon Reader Service please send £1.90 per title to: Mills & Boon Reader Service, Freepost, P.O. Box 236, Croydon, Surrey, CR9 9EL, quote your Subscriber No:.................................. (if applicable) and complete the name and address details below. Alternatively, these books are available from many local Newsagents including W H Smith, J Menzies, Martins and other paperback stockists from 12 August 1994.

Name:..
Address:...
....Post Code:........................

To Retailer: If you would like to stock M&B books please contact your regular book/magazine wholesaler for details.

You may be mailed with offers from other reputable companies as a result of this application.
If you would rather not take advantage of these opportunities please tick box. ☐

SUMMER SPECIAL!

Four exciting new Romances for the price of three

Each Romance features British heroines and their encounters with dark and desirable Mediterranean men. *Plus, a free Elmlea recipe booklet inside every pack.*

So sit back and enjoy your sumptuous summer reading pack and indulge yourself with the free Elmlea recipe ideas.

Available July 1994   Price £5.70

MILLS & BOON

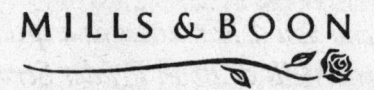

Available from WH Smith, John Menzies, Volume One, Forbuoys, Martins, Woolworths, Tesco, Asda, Safeway and other paperback stockists. Also available from Mills & Boon Reader Service, FREEPOST, PO Box 236, Croydon, Surrey CR9 9EL. (UK Postage & Packing free)

4 FREE
Romances and 2 FREE gifts just for you!

You can enjoy all the heartwarming emotion of true love for FREE! Discover the heartbreak and happiness, the emotion and the tenderness of the modern relationships in Mills & Boon Romances.

We'll send you 4 Romances as a special offer from Mills & Boon Reader Service, along with the opportunity to have 6 captivating new Romances delivered to your door each month.

laim your FREE books and gifts overleaf...

An irresistible offer from Mills & Boon

Become a regular reader of Romances with Mills & Boon Reader Service and we'll welcome you with 4 books, a CUDDLY TEDDY and a special MYSTERY GIFT all absolutely FREE.

And then look forward to receiving 6 brand new Romances each month, delivered to your door hot off the presses, postage and packing FREE! Plus our free Newsletter featuring author news, competitions, special offers and much more.

This invitation comes with no strings attached. You may cancel or suspend your subscription at any time, and still keep your free books and gifts.

It's so easy. Send no money now. Simply fill in the coupon below and post it to -
Reader Service, FREEPOST, PO Box 236, Croydon, Surrey CR9 9EL.

NO STAMP REQUIRED

Free Books Coupon

Yes! Please rush me 4 FREE Romances and 2 FREE gifts! Please also reserve me a Reader Service subscription. If I decide to subscribe I can look forward to receiving 6 brand new Romances for just £11.40 each month, postage and packing FREE. If I decide not to subscribe I shall write to you within 10 days - I can keep the free books and gifts whatever I choose. I may cancel or suspend my subscription at any time. I am over 18 years of age.

Ms/Mrs/Miss/Mr _____ EP71R

Address _____

_____

Postcode _____ Signature _____

Offers closes 31st October 1994. The right is reserved to refuse an application and change the terms of this offer. One application per household. Offer not available for current subscribers to Mills & Boon Romances. Offer only valid in UK and Eire. Overseas readers please write for details. Southern Africa write to IBS Private Bag X3010, Randburg 2125. You may be mailed with offers from other reputable companies as a result of this application. Please tick box if you would prefer not to receive such offers. ☐

mps MAILING PREFERENCE SERVICE